Herman Lilienthal Lonsdale

Lent, past and present

a study of the primitive origin of Lent, its purpose and usages

Herman Lilienthal Lonsdale

Lent, past and present
a study of the primitive origin of Lent, its purpose and usages

ISBN/EAN: 9783741193507

Manufactured in Europe, USA, Canada, Australia, Japa

Cover: Foto ©Andreas Hilbeck / pixelio.de

Manufactured and distributed by brebook publishing software
(www.brebook.com)

Herman Lilienthal Lonsdale

Lent, past and present

INTRODUCTORY NOTE.

MUCH has been written on the history of Lent, its purpose, its uses and abuses. And still there is room for more, and the present volume is intended to meet what is believed to be a popular want.

There is always danger that any positive ordinance, or any institution may come to be considered as an end in itself, and not as a means to a great moral end. In such case, the means are in the first place exaggerated, and then in the reaction the means are disparaged and, oftentimes, abandoned. It is a matter of the utmost importance to keep the balance true between these two extremes, and it seems to me this is accomplished in the following pages.

Besides this, the whole "study," as the writer modestly terms it, contains a vast amount of useful information, presented in a plain and attractive way ; information that cannot fail of being practically useful.

I gladly and cordially commend this volume to the careful attention of those who desire to understand the history and uses of an institution which is to-day commended and, to a certain extent imitated in quarters where it was once strongly denounced.

J. WILLIAMS.

Middletown, Conn.,
   August 17, 1894.

PREFACE.

THE present book has grown out of the needs of the writer ministering in a suburban parish, to investigate more fully the early origin of Lent, its purpose and primitive usages; and inasmuch as he knows of no single work which covers exactly the same ground, he ventures to hope the present publication will not be found unnecessary.

The Lectures here printed were delivered as Sermons on the Sunday mornings of last Lent, which will account for the instances of direct address. These by advice have been retained.

The general title of the book, "LENT—PAST AND PRESENT," will indicate its scope. Not only are the primitive origin, the purpose, and the usages of Lent traced, but an attempt has also been made to apply to our times the principles underlying the institution of Lent.

It is hoped that this book will be found helpful to clergymen pressed for time ; to lay readers who may wish to give connected instructions during Lent on its origin, etc., to the congregations under their charge ; and also to earnest laymen and laywomen who desire to know more of the early origin and usages of Lent than is generally known.

Owing to the popular character of the book it has been deemed inexpedient to give footnote references for the many quotations. It is needless to say that the author is under deepest obligations to Bingham's *Antiquities ;* and among many more authorities to such fathers as St. Chrysostom and St. Augustine.

The pleasant duty remains to the author to here publicly express his thanks to the Presiding Bishop of the Church, who has most kindly written an Introductory Note ; also for the great privilege which during three years the writer enjoyed of the reverend prelate's instructions, and for many other kindnesses since continued.

H. L.

Wethersfield, Conn.,
August 22, 1894.

CONTENTS.

I.

THE PRIMITIVE ORIGIN OF LENT.

II.

THE PRIMITIVE PURPOSE OF LENT.

III.

LENTEN OBSERVANCES.

Contents.

IV.

FASTING.

V.

HOLY WEEK.

VI.

HOLY WEEK.

I.

THE PRIMITIVE ORIGIN OF LENT.

LENT—PAST AND PRESENT.

I.

THE PRIMITIVE ORIGIN OF LENT.

One man esteemeth one day above another: another esteemeth every day alike. Let every man be fully persuaded in his own mind. *Romans* xiv. 5.

IN the Christian world to-day there is such a variety of usage as to fasts and festivals, or to absence of them altogether, that the minds of many might easily be confused as to their validity or utility. One Christian body claims right for its usage, another for its usage, and still another would claim liberty to observe no day of festival or fast whatsoever.

What then in the face of this diversity are we to do? The course most reasonable to take for our guidance seems to be the apostolic precept " Let every man be fully persuaded in

his own mind." We may premise at the out-
set that we have nothing to do with the usages
of other Christian bodies. We are concerned
with our own festivals and fasts. Are we, however, fully persuaded as to their authority and
their utility? If we are faithful communicants
we will in all probability accept the usages of
the Church of which we are members. Yet,
notwithstanding the Church's appointment of
festival and fast, we wish also to know, if we
can, the reasons for such appointment, that
when we are questioned by others who keep
not our days and esteem them not as we do, we
may be able to give an answer; yes, a reasonable answer, to him who questions us. For our
own sake, to confirm us in our attachment to
our own observances, and also for the sake of
those who know nothing of our Church and her
ways, we wish and ought to be fully instructed
and fully established.

It will be my purpose, therefore, during the
Sunday mornings of this Lenten season to
study with you the origin, purpose and observ-

ance of Lent.   I shall endeavor to study the subject historically, forming no theories, and twisting no facts to fit theories.   If theories do not agree with facts then theories must go. Any study to be worth anything must be honest.   We must not form opinions and then try to fit facts to these opinions.   We will endeavor neither to stretch statements nor curtail them.   Thus only shall we reach any result that will be at all satisfactory.   The search, and the end of all inquiring is truth.   Knowledge itself is of value only in so far as it leads to truth; and even faith is worthless only as it leads to God.

To-day we will consider the institution of the Lenten fast—its early origin, duration, gradual extension, and by whom instituted.

I.   But first let us consider several of the names of the Lenten fast.

The earliest name given to this fasting season seems to be Quadragesima—the Latin equivalent for the Greek term—or the Quadragesimal Fast, referring to its length, "but whether for its being a fast of forty days or only forty hours " is a point on which differ-ence of opinion has existed.

Another name given to this season is the Ante-Paschal Fast, referring to the fact that " from the very first age it was customary to fast before Easter "—the paschal feast or pass-over.

Still another name is the one with which we are most familiar, *viz.* Lent. This name of the season is supposed to be " derived from the old English word for Spring ' Lencten, ' meaning perhaps, the time when the days lengthen."

Not to enter into a more detailed examina-tion we have these three names : Quadrages-ima, referring to the length of the fast whether according to hours or days ; Ante-Paschal fast, referring to the position of the fast in the Christian year ; and Lent, referring to its posi-tion in the natural year.

II.   Having considered some of the names of the season, we are now ready to consider the origin of Lent.   The earliest reference we have to it is in a letter preserved by Eusebius in his Church History.   Eusebius, who was born about the year 260 A. D., quotes in his history (Book v. ch. 24) a passage from a letter of Irenæus, Bishop of Lyons in Gaul, to Victor, Bishop of Rome.   The letter·was written in reference to the diversity of usage of keeping Easter in the primitive Church, and incidentally the fact is brought out of the observance of Lent.   " For the controversy," writes Irenæus, " is not only concerning the day (*i. e.* Easter) but also concerning the very manner of the fast (*i. e.* the fast before Easter).   For some think that they should fast one day, others two, yet others more ; some moreover count their day as consisting of forty hours, day and night.   And this variety in its observance has not originated in our time, but long before in that of our ancestors."   Now Irenæus, the writer of this letter, was born about the year 130 A. D., and had sat at the feet of Polycarp, who was himself a disciple of St.

John. This is what Irenæus says of Polycarp :
" Polycarp was instructed by apostles, and con-
versed with many who had seen Christ; and
I saw him in my early youth." " I can recall
the very place where Polycarp used to sit and
teach, his manner of speech, his mode of life,
his appearance, the style of his address to the
people, and the accounts which he gave of his
intercourse with (St.) John and with the others
who had seen the Lord; how he used to repeat
from memory their discourses, and the things
which he had heard from them concerning our
Lord, His miracles, and His teaching." And
in addition he says, " These things being told
me by the mercy of God, I listened to them
attentively, noting them down, not on paper,
but in my heart."

I am particular to observe this connection of
Irenæus with Polycarp because it gives us a
hint how early must have been the origin of a
Lenten fast. Irenæus was a disciple of Poly-
carp, and Polycarp was a disciple of St. John.
By spiritual descent we might say Irenæus was

a spiritual grandson of the beloved disciple St. John. In this letter to Victor we further notice, the writer says of the observance of Lent, it "has not originated in our time; but long before in that of our ancestors." Now as Polycarp was the teacher of Irenæus, we may safely say that a Lenten fast must have been observed as early as the time of this teacher, and this teacher lived in the later years of St. John the apostle. Again, if "ancestors" refers back to more than one generation, we have then the Lenten fast referred back to St. John, the teacher of Irenæus. It seems reasonable and worthy of credit therefore, that some Lenten or ante-paschal fast was an established custom at least as early as the beginning of the second century, and perhaps earlier, at the close of the first century in the last years of the beloved disciple himself.

The place of institution of this fast, connecting it as we do with St. John, was, we may believe, in the East, in Ephesus and the cities adjacent.

Again, we have evidence of the early origin of the Lenten fast in the writings of Tertullian, who lived in the second and third centuries, and who after his perversion to Montanism, in controversy with the primitive Church about fasts, chides it for keeping only the two days before Easter. We hear again of the observance of Lent by the allusion of the First General Council held in 325 A. D., and the reference to Lent by this Council tends to confirm us in the belief that this season had already been long established. In the fifth canon of this Council concerning excommunication, in order that this discipline may not be arbitrarily exercised, it is advised that two synods be held in a year when questions of discipline might be reviewed. In determining the time when these synods shall be held the canon says, "Let one synod be held before Lent," or, according to the Latinized form of the original Greek, before the Quadragesimal Fast.

After this First Council had concluded its

deliberations the Emperor Constantine wrote an encyclical letter to the bishops of the Church urging uniformity in the observance of Easter, and from this letter we indirectly learn of the universal practice of an ante-paschal fast. Thus the Emperor writes, " Let your pious sagacity, (*i. e.* the bishop) reflect how evil and improper it is, that days devoted by some to fasting should be spent by others in convivial feasting; and that after the paschal feast, some are rejoicing in festivals and relaxations, while others give themselves up to the appointed fasts." By the year 325 A. D. we may say the observance of the Lenten fast was universal in the Church. Its earliest origin, as we have seen, may reach as far back as to the later years of the apostle St. John; but if this early date be questioned, then certainly to the generation of Christians immediately succeeding the apostle one of whose disciples was Polycarp. We may safely say that a Lenten or ante-paschal fast of some kind has been observed continuously in the Christian Church

from the beginning of the second century down
to our time.

III. We have already seen from the letter
of Irenæus that there was a difference of usage
as to the time of keeping, and also as to the
length of the fast. Let us now observe what
was presumably the original duration of the
fast, and how it has been developed to its
present length.

The early historians notice diversity of
usage in regard to the fast; still they lead us to
think that originally the Lenten fast was but
forty hours long, begun about twelve on Friday
before Easter, *i. e.* Good Friday, and continued
till Sunday morning, the time of our Saviour's
resurrection. Irenæus, whom we have already
mentioned, refers to this fast as "the fast of
forty hours before Easter." It perhaps is only
right to notice that a difference of punctuation
of this passage from Irenæus gives us a different interpretation, *viz.* that the fast was of
forty days, but the general concensus of modern
scholars interpreting with the light of the his-

torical development of this season thrown upon this passage, favors the rendering "forty hours" rather than "forty days."

Tertullian also refers to the Lenten fast as coinciding with the two days, the time our Lord lay in the sepulchre, and his allusion to this period leads us to think that in his day the ante-paschal fast was not of more than forty hours in length. We may well believe that the Church, even from apostolic times, observed this season, basing the fast, as Tertullian and others tell us, on the words of our Lord, "The days will come that the Bridegroom shall be taken from them and then shall they fast." Our examination seems so far to establish the view that at the first the Lenten fast extended only over about forty hours.

Without being able to trace the gradual increase in length of this season, we notice that by the end of the third and beginning of the fourth century the Lenten fast had greatly lengthened ; but even so, though the practice of a fast was universal, there was no absolute uniformity as to its duration. The historian Socrates writes, "One may observe how the ante-paschal fast is differently observed by men of different churches. The Romans fast three weeks before Easter, only the Sabbaths and Lord's Days excepted; the Illyrians and all Greece and the Alexandrians fast six weeks; others (*i. e.* the Church of Constantinople) begin their fast seven weeks before Easter, but only fast fifteen days by intervals."

Cassian, another historian, tells us, " Though some churches kept their Lent six weeks, and some seven, yet none of them made their fast above thirty-six days in the whole." Yet notwithstanding the fact that the various churches had different periods for their fast, they all called it the Quadragesimal Fast. So the name Quadragesima is by no means proof positive of the belief of some, that the fast was always one of forty days. In fact, as we have just seen, Cassian says none " made their fast above thirty-six days in the whole," and the reason given for this period of observance was that it was one tenth of the year, a tithe of time which should be devoted to God. As Christians tithed their alms so should they tithe their year.

But the variation in the number of weeks kept by different churches leads us to consider the way in which the fast was computed. Thus those who kept six weeks reckoned only thirty-six days for their fast, for from the forty-two days of six weeks was deducted the six Sundays, thus leaving but thirty-six days. Again, those churches which kept seven weeks kept only thirty-six fasting days: for though seven weeks give us forty-nine days, yet all the Saturdays—the Saturday before Easter being excepted—as well as Sundays were taken out; thus thirteen days were deducted from the forty-nine days, which still made the fast one of thirty-six days. It was the Eastern Church rather than the Western which kept a greater number of weeks, because in the Eastern Church Saturday—the great Sabbath excepted—has never been a fast day, not even in the

Lenten season. This accounts for the Lenten fast beginning earlier in the Eastern than in the Western Church, and so lasting through a greater number of weeks, though the actual number of fasting days was the same.

It is interesting to observe the reason given by St. Chrysostom for the exception of Saturdays and Sundays from fasting. "As there are stations," says he, "and inns in the public roads, for weary travellers to refresh themselves, and rest from their labors, that they may more cheerfully go on again in their journey; and as in the sea there are shores and havens for seamen to betake themselves to, when they are in a storm, and refresh themselves from the violence of the winds, and then begin sailing again; so the Lord hath appointed these two days (Saturday and Sunday) in the week, as stations, and inns, and shores, and havens, for those to rest in who have taken upon them the course of fasting in this holy time of Lent, that they may refresh their bodies a little from the labor of fasting, and recreate their minds, and after the two days are past, to go on again with cheerfulness in the journey which they have begun."

But to return to the extension of this season the next advance is to the exact period of forty days which now prevails throughout western Christendom. ˊ Who added Ash-Wednesday and the three days following it to the beginning of Lent in the Western Church so as to make the season exactly forty days is not unanimously agreed upon by historians.ˊ "Some say it was the work of Gregory the Great, but others ascribe it to Gregory II., who lived over a hundred years later." But whichever of these Bishops added the four extra days, they are an addition made to the season some time after it had been an established usage of the Church to observe a Lenten fast, as Cassian has told us, of only thirty-six days. If the four extra days were added by Gregory I., the Lent fast of forty days would not be earlier than the close of the sixth or beginning of the seventh century. If the change was made by Gregory II., then the practice of a Lent fast of forty days does not antedate 715 A. D.

But we may see a reason for the change from thirty-six days—the tithe of the year—to forty days. Forty days is a period that occurs frequently in the Bible as a time of fasting and prayer. Moses when first he went up into the mount to receive the Law says of himself, "I abode in the mount forty days and forty nights. I neither did eat bread nor drink water." Again he says of himself after he had broken the two Tables of the Law because of the idolatry of his people, "And I fell down before the Lord as at the first, forty-days and forty nights, I did neither eat bread nor drink water, because of all your sins which ye sinned." So too it is inferred by many that Elijah fasted forty days after he had twice eaten of food prepared for him by an angel, "and went in the strength of that meat forty days and forty nights unto Horeb the mount of God." Briefly to instance a few more Old Testament examples of this number forty: "This was the number of days God covered the earth with the deluge; this the number of years in which the children of Israel did penance in the wilderness; and the Ninevites had this number of days allowed for their repentance." But chiefly is the parallel found in the life of our Lord, who, led up of the spirit into the wilderness to be tempted of the devil, "fasted forty days and forty nights." The change then which was made from thirty-six to forty days we may believe was based on the scriptural analogies which have been quoted, and which at the same time made the number of days agree with the name of the season itself—Quadragesima—a name which notwithstanding the variation in the length of the season in different sections of the primitive Church, was indifferently applied.

It may not be amiss to briefly state how the forty days' fast is computed. Ash-Wednesday to Easter—a period of six weeks and four days—gives us forty-six days, from which number of days are subtracted the six Sundays in Lent, thus giving us the Lenten fast of forty days.

Here too a word may be permitted as to the origin of the word Ash-Wednesday. We have learned that originally there was no Ash-Wednesday connected with the Lenten fast. This day was not added, at the earliest, until the time of Gregory I., and it derives its name from the custom which was instituted at the time the day was added of sprinkling ashes upon the heads of penitents to remind them of their mortality. Further, as to this practice we are led to believe that ashes were not sprinkled upon all the worshippers, but only on the heads of those who were penitents, and were under sentence of ecclesiastical discipline.

IV. We are now in a position to come to the question of the institution of the fast. Is it of divine, apostolic, or ecclesiastical institution? As to its divine institution we may perhaps say that if the word divine is limited to verbal scriptural precept, then the fast as we observe it to-day cannot claim for itself divine institution. Next we ask what is meant by apostolic institution? If by this term be meant a posi-

tive precept of the apostles, again we may say
that there is no such direct injunction left to
us. Further, the widely varying length of the
fast in the early Church would also preclude
any apostolical directions. There is left then the
third alternative—the ecclesiastical institution
of this fast. Historically we notice that "from
the first age of the Christian Church it was
customary to fast before Easter," a custom
which may be reasonably supposed to be
derived from scriptural precedent and apostolic practice, yet without positive scriptural or
apostolic injunction. St. Augustine's summary
of the question may assist us here. He says,
that "the authority and foundation which the
Lent-fast has out of the Gospel, is the same that
it has out of the Old Testament, which was not
any precept, but the example of Moses and
Elias. And second, that the Lent-fast is owing
to the councils of the fathers and the custom
of the Church, in like manner as the eight days
of the neophytes and the fifty days of Pentecost owe their observation to the same

original." This clearly points to the ecclesiastical institution of the Lenten-fast. To sum up, we may say that the fact of some fast of varying length before Easter has since apostolic days been observed in God's Church; but that its duration is nowhere definitely laid down, this detail being left to the several churches. But little by little changes were made until at the last in the Western Church either in the seventh or eighth century the season practically as we observe it to-day was fixed.

V. Let me now in closing briefly summarize what we have gathered from our study of the origin of Lent.

Some fast can be traced to the beginning of the second century if not to the close of the first, and so would seem to be of apostolic practice and perhaps precept, though we have no authentic record of its apostolic institution.

This fast has among other appellations been known by the names of Quadragesima, the Ante-Paschal Fast, and Lent.

Its length has varied, extending at the first

presumably from Good Friday and ending Easter morning—about forty hours. In time this period was lengthened to thirty-six days, and still later in the seventh or eighth century to forty days.

To draw now a few practical conclusions, if anyone should ask me "Why do you keep Lent? seeing that you yourself acknowledge there is no direct scriptural injunction therefor," my answer would be that since the days of the apostles the Church of God throughout the world has observed a fast preceding Easter. Its length I grant has varied, but now for about 1300 years in Western Christendom ecclesiastical usage has adopted a period of forty days. And this time—set apart for a special season of fasting, penitence, prayer and almsgiving, which in God's providence and mercy has during all the past centuries been blessed by Him as a season of conviction and devotion, of repentance and pardon for the many millions of the sons and daughters of men who have gone before—will I believe be blessed to-day to me and to all others who will in the spirit of the holy men and women of old afflict ourselves in like manner, make like humble confession of sins, and come and kneel in the divine presence for pardon and peace. What nourished and brought up saints of old will I believe be found equally able to bring up and nourish saints in these latter days of this nineteenth century ; and so I accept the season of Lent as the Church's appointment for my spiritual needs and wants and for my spiritual edification and sanctification. " The Church is holier than the holiest of its members, and likewise is wiser than the wisest of her members." And because the spiritual needs of men and women to-day are just as pressing as in the earliest day of the Christian Church and Christian life, because we sin the same sins, and are in need of like penitence as the men and women of old, and because what can be done at any time is usually done at no time, I as a loyal son and member accept this stated definite provision of the Church for a special

season of penitence and prayer not only for the
whole Church, but also for me individually.
And because, brethren, your needs are the
same as mine, I commend this present season
of Lent to your acceptance, in order that you
too by special and sincere self-examination, by
increased prayer, and by deeper penitence may
go on from strength to strength, and increase
in grace and holiness, without which we none
shall see the Lord.

II.

The Primitive Purpose of Lent.

II.

THE PRIMITIVE PURPOSE OF LENT.

For the time is come that judgment must begin at the house of God. 1 *Peter* iv. 17.

THE history of the origin of Lent, when instituted, and the gradual lengthening of the season, we have already considered. We now come to the consideration of the object or purpose of its institution. Why was the Lenten season established and what was its aim? This is the question we shall now endeavor to answer.

I. The primary reason we find to be the mourning for the death and burial of the Saviour—the remembrance of which naturally occurred to the Church when it made preparation for celebrating the joyful feast of the Resurrection. As it has been said, the reason for the original institution was due to " the apostles' fasting at this time, because the Bridegroom (their Lord) was taken away from them." " In compliance with which practice, the ancients generally observed those two days in which our Saviour lay in the grave " as a season of mourning. " Of this mourning Lent is the perpetual reminder." From this earliest of reasons that has been given by Church historians for the observance of Lent, we incidentally learn that primitively—at least in the latter part of the first or beginning of the second century—the Lenten fast had no connection or reference to our Lord's fast of forty days in the wilderness. It was later, when the season of Lent had been lengthened, that the connection with our Lord's fast and temptation was advanced. The first reason then for the establishment of this season was connected with the Saviour's crucifixion and burial, not with his earlier life and temptation. · " The primary object of the institution of a fast before Easter was doubtless that of perpetuating in the hearts of every generation of Christians, the sorrow and the mourning which the apostles and disciples felt during the time that the Bridegroom was taken away from them."

II. This fast of forty hours or two days was at a time however when Christian fervor was deep and lasting. "And so long," says Cassian, "as the perfection of the primitive Church remained inviolable there was no observation of Lent [as a period of self-discipline, which is now the radical thought connected with the season.] But when the multitude of believers began to depart from apostolic devotion, and brood continually upon their riches; when, instead of imparting them to the common use of all, they labored only to lay them up and augment them for their own private expenses; then it seemed good to all bishops, by a canonical indiction of fasts, to recall men to holy works, who were bound with secular cares, and had almost forgotten what continency and compunction meant; and to compel them by the necessity of a law, to dedicate the tenth of their time to God." In this statement of Cassian we may notice the undesigned evidence for the ecclesiastical institution of the Lenten fast in its later form. The reason then given by Cassian for the institution of the fast is the loss of apostolic fervor and devotion. This decline took place so soon as the Church became connected with the State. When the alliance between the Church and the Empire was formed, the lust of the world crept into the Church. The Master had said, " My kingdom is not of this world," but his professed disciples, many of them in high places, preferred not to accept or else to disregard this truth. They clutched at temporal power when it came within their reach. When the Church was persecuted by Emperors and officials, and by law, then the Church was pure. Because then as a rule no one would venture to declare himself a Christian who was not so from stern inward conviction and moral necessity, when he knew that such declaration involved the

flames, the cross, the lions, banishment, impri-
sonment. To be a Christian when the Emperors were heathen and frowned upon and
persecuted the Church, meant the readiness
and willingness to sacrifice not only property
but life, family, and everything that man holds
dear in this world. The ante-Nicene Church,
therefore, was in a measure pure and devoted,
consistent and spiritual. But when the
Emperor Constantine declared in favor of
Christianity; and the Christian religion from
being one of the proscribed and persecuted
faiths—*fides illicitæ*—was honored above all
others; then multitudes hastened to join the
Church, not because of inward conviction, not
because of moral necessity, not because of
devotion to Christ, but because the Church
meant for them possible imperial favor, aggran-
disement, worldly prosperity, outward success,
political honor. Men of no moral convictions
were willing to profess adherence to the Christian faith, and thus courtiers, libertines, politi-
cians, and profligates, all were willing to submit

to the Church if thereby their several aims were advanced. It was necessary, therefore, to enforce by ecclesiastical injunction some substitute for the civil persecution which was now a thing past and gone. Persecution had preserved the Church in purity. The fires of martyrdom had refined the Church of dross. Something, even though immeasurably inadequate, had to take the place of persecution in order to maintain the primitive purity. There was but one course, that was to impose a season of self-discipline on all Christians. No time was more fitting than the fast before Easter. Here too we see a reason why in the growing worldliness and corruption of the Church the season of mourning and fasting which in the sub-apostolic Church was presumably but forty hours long, had to be increased to thirty-six and at last to forty days. The need of some severe self-discipline to purify the Church called for a lengthened Lenten fast.

III. As the Church through imperial favor

and alliance grew impure and lost its apostolic
fervor, we can readily see how this loss of zeal
would react on the devotions and worship of its
members. There is much dispute, and at best
uncertainty, whether it ever was the custom
of the Church to observe a daily communion.
Authorities are to be found for and against
such observance. This practice we might say
was in some part of the Church observed, and
perhaps also for some time, but never we think
universally and for all time. But I think it
may be conceded that the primitive Church
observed a weekly communion, through the
period of its purity, and not only was the offering made weekly, but all Christians communicated weekly. With the loss of devotion, even
though the communion was weekly administered, yet all Christians did not as formerly
partake weekly. Their loss of zeal, their loss
of devotion, their lukewarmness caused many
to abstain altogether from the Lord's Table, or
to approach it as rarely as possible. It became
the custom by degrees for some " to communi-

cate chiefly at Easter "; for others to communicate " at no other time but that only." Accordingly the Lenten fast before Easter was appointed as a time for special preparation for communion at Easter, that " by proper and spiritual exercises those might be duly prepared to receive the communion at Easter, who could not be prevailed upon to frequent it at other seasons." St. Chrysostom says of this reason, " Because men were used to come indevoutly and inconsiderately to the communion, especially at Easter, therefore the Fathers, considering the mischiefs arising from such careless approaches met together, and appointed forty days of fasting : that in these days men, being carefully purified by prayer, and almsdeeds, and fasting, and watching, and tears, and confession of sins, and other like exercises, might come with a pure conscience to the holy table." So again in another place to the same purpose this Father says, " As they that take great pains to run in a race, reap no advantage if they fail of the prize ; so we have no benefit from all the labor and pains we bestow upon fasting, unless we can come with a pure conscience to partake of the holy table. For this end we use fasting, and Lent, and assemblies for so many days together, and hearing, and praying, and preaching ; that by our diligence in the use of these means, and regard to the Divine commands, we may wipe off the sins of the whole year that stick to us, and so with spiritual boldness and reverence partake of the unbloody sacrifice."/ If this be so do we not gather a hint for our own con-duct ? If the Lenten fast was established in the early Church as a preparation for commun-ion at Easter; if all the preaching, services, prayer, fasting, almsgiving were to be means of preparation ; then we see how to-day those of us who expect to communicate at Easter should make use of the Lenten season, how we should take advantage of the opportunitie of the services provided, the opportunities of almsgiving and deeds of mercy and charity which are also offered. Let me say as did the

sainted Chrysostom of old, the Lenten season
is given us for one reason at least, as a time of
preparation for our Easter communion; we are
to be made ready by the pains which we now
take to come then with a pure conscience:
how then I ask can any come on that great
festival who neglect the means of preparation
now offered at this time of Lent. Consider
this you who propose to come to the communion at Easter, and yet think you may neglect
the preparation therefor which the Church during this season affords you.

IV. Once more, the Lenten fast was made use
of—if not originally so designed—in later centuries as the special time for preparing catechumens or candidates for their baptism on
Easter-even. True it is that in the days of
the apostles as also with us to-day, baptism
was administered at any time. Candidates
were not put off by the apostles, but just so
soon as they were prepared they baptized
them. This is proven by the baptism of about
3000 on the first Whitsunday. Again, we

notice that the Evangelist Philip after duly preaching Christ to the Eunuch, when they come to some water is asked by him saying, "See, here is water : what doth hinder one to be baptized?" And believing, he is baptized. So too this same Philip preaching in Samaria converts many men and women who believing were baptized. It would be possible to multiply examples to prove that in the apostolic Church men and women were baptized as soon as they professed their belief that Jesus is the Son of God. Yet in course of time it became the practice in the early Church to defer baptism—except in case of extreme sickness—to Epiphany, Easter, and Pentecost ; but of these three times of baptism Easter was the most celebrated. The reason perhaps why this delay in baptism was ordered seems to be due in great measure to that root of evil which troubled the Church after her connection with the State, *viz.* the loss of piety, and fervor, and the creeping in of a worldly spirit. Accordingly it seemed best to make catechumens wait, "to proceed more slowly with the candidates of baptism, both in the instruction and the trial of them because of their dulness, and negligence, and frequent relapses." The season of Lent, therefore, became the special season set apart for the instruction of the candidates in the Christian faith. But not only was there at this time something for teachers to do, the candidates themselves were required to pray, and with fasting to beg of God remission of sins. Cyril of Jerusalem, who has left to us some of his catechetical lectures given to catechumens for baptism, thus addresses them concerning Lent : "The present season is a season of confession, all worldly cares are to be laid aside, for you strive for your souls. You that have been busy about the things of the world, and troubled in vain so many years, will ye not bestow forty days in prayer for the salvation of your souls?" Thus one of the purposes of this Lenten season was for the special preparation of catechumens for their Easter baptism.

V. But this fast of Lent served still another

purpose. And we see how in this case also the reason is due to the loss of purity of the Church owing to its alliance with the State. This other purpose was that Lent should be a season of special preparation for penitents who looked for re-admission into the Church at Easter. It was a few days before this great feast that offenders, those who were under ecclesiastical discipline, were absolved after a season of penitence and prayer. "Lent was always more strictly observed by them, as a decent preparation for the absolution they then expected." The discipline of this season for penitents was one of rigor, involving fasting, prayer, and a strict observance of the rules laid down for their conduct. For forty days they gave evidence of the sincerity of their repentance and submission in hopes of being restored to the assembly of the faithful, to receive absolution, and also to be admitted to the communion. On this custom Gregory of Nyssa has said, "The anniversary solemnity of Easter was not only the time of regenerating

catechumens, but of begetting those again to a
lively hope, who had forfeited it by their sins,
but were desirous to regain it by repentance
and conversion from dead works to walk again
in the paths of life."

These then were some of the reasons for
and aims of the institution of Lent—as a
reminder of our Lord's death and burial and
the mourning of the disciples ; as a season in
which to stimulate the declining fervor and
piety of the Church ; as a time of special preparation for the reception of the Communion
at Easter; as the period during which catechumens were instructed in the Faith, and themselves exercised self-discipline by fasting,
prayer, and almsgiving preparatory to baptism
at Easter ; also as a season during which penitents by strict observance of the fast of these
days, and by other evidences of penitence
hoped to receive absolution at Easter and to
be restored to the fold and to full communion.

And now it may be asked, in the divided
state of Christendom, with such diverse condi-

tions surrounding us to-day, do the same reasons hold, do the same purposes remain for observing Lent; do we have like aims? We reply, if all the specific reasons of the early Church do not remain valid, yet some of them do, and certainly the principles which lay at the bottom of all those reasons still hold true. It is evident that the discipline exercised by the primitive Church has in these later centuries failed. Were we now to say to an offender that unless he gave evidence of penitence for some scandalous offence he would be disciplined or excommunicated, I venture to think he would not mind the threat. Old things, and old discipline have passed away. So, too, the usages have varied. We no longer delay baptism, but administer the sacrament whenever requested, and when the candidate—if adult—is sufficiently instructed. But notwithstanding the loss of ancient discipline, and also the change of usage, the root principle which caused a lengthening of the fast from forty hours to forty days still remains to be consid-

ered, *viz.* the decline of fervor, devotion and
piety, in the Church and in its members. | The
same reason that accounted for this loss in the
fourth century, accounts for it to-day, *viz.* the
strong désire to unite the service of the world
and of God, to make God's kingdom a kingdom of this world, in direct opposition to the
statement of our Lord. And because of the
loss of fervor and devotion we need to-day
just as much as the Church did fifteen centuries ago to appoint a special season, during
which by increased zeal in God's house, by
self-denial, by self-discipline, by fasting, by
prayers, by almsgiving to arouse the whole
Church and each individual member of it to
the great need of a closer walk with God, and
a heartier consecration of self and self's belong-
ings to Him.

The influence of the world on the Church
and on each of us is too apt to make us lose
sight of spiritual realities, their importance,
and their eternal value; and so little by little
we yield to the narcotic influence of the pres-

ent—be it its pleasures or gaities, its business or its duties, its hopes or its struggles, its joys or its sorrows, until we become benumbed to all higher interests and hopes, and joys and realities, until we gradually lose sight and experience of the former peace and rapture and ecstacy with which spiritual things and communion filled us. This season then has for its purpose to-day the object of meeting the spiritual needs and wants of our nature which we are certain to neglect if we are not specially warned and called to take heed to our ways.

" In this hallowed season then the Church, by the voice of all her holy services calleth the world to repentance from the rising of the sun to the going down thereof. And if ever there was an institution calculated to promote the glory of God, by forwarding the salvation of man, it is this appointment of a certain set time for all persons to consider their ways, to break off their sins. For though most certain it is, that sorrow should be the constant attendant on sin, and daily transgressions call for daily penitence; yet fatal experience convinces us of another truth no less certain, that in a body so frail, and a world so corrupt, care and pleasures soon oppress the heart, and insensibility brings on the slumbers of listlessness and negligence as to its spiritual concerns, which unless dissipated and dispersed by frequently repeated admonitions, will at length seal it up in the deep sleep of a final impenitence. It was wisely foreseen that, should the sinner be permitted to reserve for himself the choice of a 'convenient season' wherein to turn from sin to righteousness, that 'convenient season' would never come; and the specious plea of keeping every day holy alike, would often be found to cover a design of keeping none holy at all."

You know, brethren, the deceitfulness of the heart, you know the cares of this life are apt to choke the good seed, you know that what spiritual life you do possess is only maintained by a constant struggle, you know too that at no time in the life of the Church of God is she called on to contend with her rival, the world, so strongly and fiercely as now for the souls of men, you know what mighty allurements and fascinations the world is perpetually offering to the minds and bodies of men to dazzle them and to bewilder them, to sensualize them, and to cause them to renounce God;—if so, then there is no time in the history of the Christian Church for its own sake and struggle for existence, and also for the souls committed to her care and for the souls of all men, when a set period of fasting and prayers is more needed than now in these last years of this fast fleeing century. We are threatened by godlessness, atheism, materialism and all the hydra-headed isms, which clamor for recognition; in most insinuating forms the adversary of souls is tempting us; surely now is no time to throw away the smallest weapon of defence we may possess, certainly not this one of the season of Lent, which the Church for now these many centuries has found to be a means of reviving the sluggish, careless and indifferent souls of her children, reanimating their piety, increasing their fervor, and leading them to a higher plane of service and devotion not only to God but also to man. Nay! we need if possible to hold more firmly than ever to this observance of the Lenten fast, that we fail not in our duty, that we lose not our own souls, that we miss not eternal life. Divine Providence has in the past guided the Church to observe this season, and we believe that because of the likeness of the needs and wants of men and women to-day to that of their forebears, Divine Providence will enable the Church to maintain this holy season, until at last all seasons will be holy, when this Church now militant shall become the Church triumphant and in God's presence we shall have peace, and light, and joy forevermore.

III.

LENTEN OBSERVANCES.

III.

LENTEN OBSERVANCES.

He that regardeth the day, regardeth it unto the Lord:
and he that regardeth not the day, to the Lord he doth
not regard it. *Rom*. xiv. 6.

THESE words of the apostle give us the
hint that the observance of days might
vary, and yet the Lord honored. St. Paul
points to a great truth which he so frequently
dwells upon in his teaching, *viz.* that in the body
of Christ there is diversity of gifts, adminis-
trations and operations, yet it is the same Spirit
that worketh all in all. Liberty in Christ he
desires to maintain not only for himself, but
also for others. If in the Christian world to-day
there was more of that ancient Pauline spirit
of liberty, there would be I think a great deal
more of Christian unity, and also Church unity.

We hear high-sounding phrases such as "in essentials unity, in non-essentials liberty, in all things charity," and yet this great sentiment is practically worthless in numberless cases because we are so determined to overlap essentials and non-essentials. We are not willing, Christians though we call ourselves, to be content to refer to the Word of God for essentials. But one here and another there goes about to establish his or her righteousness —one church or denomination here and another there determines this to be essential which another deems non-essential, and thus because of the elastic and undetermined limits of essentials and non-essentials—not only is there no unity or liberty, but even the greatest virtue of all—charity itself—is lacking.

Ah! will the day ever come when the Body of Christ, " the company of all faithful people " shall be healed of its schisms and its sores, and Christians everywhere shall call their fellow Christians brother, sister !

From the text we learn that the great

apostle among even his converts recognizes the
individuality of man, and provides for their
differences. He will not compel all to conform
to one mould. They shall not all speak after
the same manner. He knows this is an impossibility. He knows it is directly opposed
to divine truth and divine operation. "The
manifestation of the Spirit is given to every
man to profit withal. For to me is given by
the Spirit the word of wisdom; to another the
word of knowledge by the same Spirit; to
another faith by the same Spirit; to another
the gift of healing by the same Spirit; to
another the working of miracles; to another
prophecy; to another discerning of spirits; to
another divers kinds of tongues; to another
the interpretation of tongues; but all these
worketh that one and the self-same Spirit, divid-
ing to every man severally as he will." Thus
in practice and devotion he makes no attempt
to circumscribe the liberty of his converts by
enforcing unchangeable observances and in-
flexible rites. The great truth he inculcates is

"the kingdom of God is not meat and drink; but righteousness and peace, and joy in the Holy Ghost."

This apostolic spirit of liberty, and of diversity in unity we find maintained in the sub-apostolic church. Here great variation of usage is allowed. Liberty in Christ is an accepted and acknowledged principle, and whether the church be found in Asia Minor or Corinth, in Alexandria or Carthage, in Rome or Gaul, diversity of usage does not destroy unity of faith, nor hinder intercommunion and charity to all.

To-day in the consideration of our subject we reach the question of the observances, practices, customs, usages, rules and habits adopted or enforced by authority during Lent.

In the study of our subject we need to bear in mind the marked distinctions in the periods of the Church's life. A critical turning-point was the Nicene Council held in the year 325 A. D. The period previous to this date, church historians speak of as the ante-Nicene period;

after this date as the post-Nicene age. The ante-Nicene days present to us a church scattered over the Roman empire, with certain fundamental points of agreement, yet with many marked differences of usage. One marked difference was in the time of keeping Easter. Some churches, especially those of Asia Minor, kept Easter according to the Jewish Calendar regardless whether it fell on a Sunday or not. Other churches, more especially the Latin, kept Easter always on a Sunday. Not until the Nicene Council of 325 A. D. was there a general unanimity of practice, corresponding to the usage which prevails to-day, *viz.* of keeping Easter always on a Sunday. We see in this diversity of custom of observing Easter, the great liberty and wide difference of usage, which was allowed and asserted, accepted and adopted by different churches in the ante-Nicene period of the Church. What was true of Easter was true in like degree of nearly every other practice. Usages varied, and this is especially true of

Lent. From a letter of Irenæus which has already been referred to, we notice that the length of the Lenten season varied in different churches. The same is true of the customs and usages in connection with this season. If we think a while we see a reason for this variation of practice. Before the Nicene Council, or up to within a few years of it, the Christian faith was under nominal if not practical proscription. If any one chose to bring a complaint against a Christian as being unwilling to sacrifice to the gods, or offer incense, the official to whom the complaint was made was obliged to investigate the case and to afford the accused an opportunity to prove the falsity or truth of the charge by requiring of him to offer incense. If the Christian accused refused, he could be punished, and the severity of the punishment would often be determined by the strength of the attachment of the official to the heathen faith, or by the degree of bitterness or popular feeling and clamor against Christians at the time in the place of accusation. Occasionally, owing to famines, pestilences, drought, or any physical calamity, heathen populations would stir up enmity against Christians, accusing them as being responsible for all these disasters. Then Christians had to suffer. Again, the strength of the adherence of the Emperor to the pagan worship of the State would also determine in great measure the violence of the persecution or its leniency. In a word, whatever organization the Church had in the ante-Nicene period was to a great extent local. It could not in the face of imperial and popular opposition make an open show of its customs and usages. Thus each church holding in essentials of the faith with all other Christian churches where-ever found, and holding communion, and granting to travelling communicants letters commendatory to the faithful everywhere, was yet of necessity, because of the liability to per-secution, obliged to determine for itself in great measure its own usages and customs, adapting them to their peculiar situation and

needs and according to the circumstances of
the time, place, popular feeling.   There was no
central council to issue orders and directions.
The tendency to yield to centralized authority
was not yet in existence, because there was no
central authority.   The union of Church and
State—the foundation of centralization—was
yet future.   Local self-government was for pru-
dential reasons almost a necessity.

The alliance of the Church with the State
under Constantine in 325 A. D., gave to the
Church a political status, and an external unity
which it had hitherto lacked.   At the same
time that state recognition was accorded to
the Church, there naturally sprang up the
desire not only for external unity of communion, but also unity of usage, and uniformity
of customs and practices.   The tendency of
thought within the Church now led to centralization and some seat of authority.   The influence of the State upon the Church became
paramount, and it looked to the State for
models of its constitutions, divisions, usages.

Accordingly, after the Nicene Council we notice in all directions this tendency to unification, to a similarity of customs, seasons, festivals and fasts. We note this gradual approximation of observances in the usages of Lent. Councils now issued canons; synods prescribed practices; and with the division of the Church into patriarchates, provinces and dioceses, we see how observances would gradually approach uniformity throughout the Church.

Our consideration of the Lenten usages after they became practically uniform will necessarily be chiefly of those that prevailed after 325 A. D., when already the influence of the State and the world had begun to lower the tone of ancient piety and fervor, when already there were beginning to show themselves traces and tendencies to formality and superstition; when already the lust of authority had crept into the Church, and power was grasped after rather than love.

For the purposes of our study we may

classify the observances and usages of Lent
under three heads: I. *Ecclesiastical;* II. *Civil;*
III. *Domestic.*

I. *Ecclesiastical.* The decreasing devotion
and growing worldliness of the Church de-
manded serious consideration. The fast of
Lent therefore was made use of to increase if
possible the fervor and spirituality of all Christians. Accordingly multiplied services were
held, and sermons preached daily through
Lent, at least in large city churches and cathe-
drals. These services and sermons the people
were urged to turn to profit. It is due to
these daily Lenten services that to-day we
possess so many patristic commentaries. The
daily sermon or homily through Lent gave the
early Fathers opportunity to take up some
book of the Bible and expound it consecu-
tively. And what is more to the point, from
contemporary notices we learn that numbers
availed themselves of these biblical and devo-
tional privileges. We are led to believe from
reliable authority that crowds went daily to

hear St. Chrysostom in Antioch, and also in Constantinople. The same is true of the numbers who went to hear St. Ambrose at Milan, and St. Augustine in North Africa.

Again, not only were there daily services and sermons, but weekly the communion was administered and received, except by those who were excommunicated or who were in the class of penitents and under discipline. It has already been observed that the matter of a daily celebration is uncertain. The truth being, perhaps, that in some parts of the Church a daily celebration was the custom, in others not; again, the size of the church would enter into the consideration of the practice; and once more what might be true of a practice in later centuries would not necessarily be true of the period which we are considering. But in connection with the communion one custom observed in the Eastern Church until some time in the seventh century needs to be noticed. By a canon of the Council of Laodicea (*cir.* 365 A. D.) it was ordered "that the

Eucharist should not be offered in Lent, on any other day except the Sabbath and the Lord's Day." The reason alleged for this restriction by the Eastern Church is " that the consecration service is proper only for festivals ; and, therefore, all other days in Lent, besides Saturdays and Sundays being fast days, they did not consecrate on those days, but only communicated in the elements which had been consecrated before," or as those elements are also called, the pre-sanctified. It must be noted that this canon did not forbid communion or participation, but only the consecration of the elements on any day except Saturday and Sunday. This custom however was not adopted in the Latin Church. It "used to consecrate, as well as communicate about three in the afternoon all the days of Lent."

Once again, ecclesiastical orders of this period " forbade the celebration of all festivals of martyrs at this season, except it were on the Sabbath (*i. e.* Saturday), or upon the Lord's Day : because all festivals were days of rejoic-

ing which were not consistent with deep
humiliation and mourning belonging to a strict
and severe fast; but (inasmuch as) the Sabbath and the Lord's Day were excepted from
fasting even in Lent. . . . therefore on these
days the festivals of martyrs might be celebrated but on no other during the whole time of
Lent." There was one exception to this rigid
rule, *viz.* the feast of the Annunciation, on
which day whenever it fell in Lent, though not
on a Saturday or Sunday, there was nevertheless
a celebration.

II. *Civil observances.* The alliance of the
State with the Church reacted on the former.
This reaction is manifested in certain state and
imperial regulations and laws concerning the
conduct of business in courts, the treatment of
prisoners, the cessation of public amusements
during Lent. Thus "imperial laws forbade
all prosecution of men in criminal actions
which might bring them to corporal punishment and torture during the whole season" of
Lent. "In the forty days" so the imperial

law runs "which by the laws of religion
are solemnly observed before Easter, let the
examination and hearing of all criminal questions be superseded ; and in the holy days of
Lent, let there be no punishments of the body,
when we expect the absolution of our souls."
Thus civil enactments prescribed postpone-
ment of lawsuits in Lent, and forbade infliction
of bodily punishment such as flogging and
branding. There were other civil usages of
this season, but they will be better considered
in connection with the days of Holy Week with
which they were specially associated.

III. *Domestic usages.* Usages which were
in some cases of ecclesiastical imposition, in as
much as they refer more to the conduct of
believers at home or in society, I have preferred
to classify as domestic. The first of these
usages touching the home that call for notice
would be that of fasting and abstinence. To
consider this at all fully at the present time
would most probably tax your patience. I will
therefore reserve this usage for separate con-

sideration. Leaving then the consideration of
the usage of fasting for the present the next
domestic rule of the Church was to forbid all
celebrations of birthdays and marriages during
Lent. The reason for this prohibition was that
these festivities " being celebrated with great
tokens and solemnities of joy, with feasting
and other ceremonies of pleasure and delight,
it was not proper to keep them in the time of
fasting, as being things inconsistent, and in-
compatible with one another. And they were
to be forborne because at this time the Church
did not allow the solemnizing of the nativities
or birthdays of her martyrs, which otherwise
were of great esteem in the Church." We see
from this how if the Church forbade the celebration of saints' days through Lent, it was only
consistent that she should forbid the celebrations of the birthdays and marriages of her
ordinary members during this same season.

Once again, the Church would have all her
faithful children abstain from attending public
games, shows, races, which might be held in the

amphitheatre or circus, as being inconsistent
with the profession of penitence, humiliation,
fasting, and mourning, which was at this time
made. Of course, then as now, it was impossible
to restrain everybody from such indulgences.
Human nature is the same everywhere and at
all times. There were inconsistent, lukewarm,
or indifferent Christians then as now. There
were also those who perhaps took a delight in
doing what they were urged not to do. In one
of his Lent sermons St. Chrysostom depre-
cates and sets himself to correct if possible this
abuse of indulging in games, plays, races, etc.,
during the holy season. " When I consider,"
says he, " how at one blast of the devil ye have
forgotten all my daily admonitions, and continued discourses, and run to that pomp of
Satan, the horse race in the Circus ; with what
heart can I think of preaching to you again
who have so soon let slip all that I said before ?
This is what chiefly raises my grief, yea, my
anger and indignation, that together with my
admonition ye have cast the reverence of this

holy season of Lent out of your souls, and
thrown yourselves into the nets of the devil."
Strong words these, but the speaker was not in
the habit of mincing his words, and calling
black white, or darkness light. Once again, to
urge them to prove sincere and to show how
their inconsistent conduct gave the lie to their
profession and did harm to the Church, Chry-
ostom says, " Subdue I beseech you this wicked
and pernicious custom ; and consider that they
who run to the Circus, not only do much harm
to themselves; but are the occasion of great
scandal to others. For when the Jews and
Gentiles see you who are every day at church
to hear a sermon, come notwithstanding to the
horse race and join with them in the Circus, will
they not reckon our religion a cheat and enter-
tain the same suspicion of us all? They will
sharpen their tongues against us all, and for the
offence of a few, condemn the whole body of
Christians." How true this is to-day as well ;
and of how many professing Christians might
these words be repeated ; yet they were uttered

nearly 1500 years ago—so unchanged is human nature.

To recapitulate, we find that Lenten observances during the post-Nicene period, affected Christians in their ecclesiastical, civil and domestic relations ; that they were positive and negative directions what to do, and what not to do. We notice too how they affected the details of life, prescribing rules for the minutest circumstances. According to the thought of those early years men and women had to be directed in most of the details of the conduct of life. Large principles with diverse applications to diverse circumstances were dropping out of sight. The State in those days respected neither privacy nor individual liberty, but whenever it felt disposed intruded into, and interfered with the most sacred relations. It is scarcely to be expected that the Church, living in this atmosphere and thus environed, could escape the time spirit. We are all more or less influenced by the thought of our age, the social and intellectual atmosphere which surrounds us. So the Church, newly allied to the State, most naturally adopted for its government many of the state ideas, and was influenced by the prevailing thought and custom of the period. As a matter of course it prescribed minute directions for the conduct of individuals in all their earthly relations. To have expected anything different would be to expect the people of those days of the fourth century to think and act as those of this nineteenth century.

Now in consideration of the ancient usages of Lent and their application to our times, what shall be our attitude to them? Shall we say they are all wrong and need no attention, in fact may be treated with contempt? or shall we on the other hand observe them to the minutest particulars and reverence them because of their antiquity? Shall we ignore them altogether, or shall we observe their every jot and tittle? Thus some to-day would have the Church impose minute regulations governing the details of daily life, others would reject any imposition whatever, even of a season of Lent. The former err, I think, in trying to revive in the nineteenth century, conditions of thought and life of the fourth and fifth centuries—an impossibility because of our totally changed circumstances and environment; the latter err in that they break the continuity of life, and though right in requiring changed rules for changed circumstances, ignore the truth of the sameness of human nature in all centuries, in the nineteenth as in the first. But are these two the only alternative; implicit acceptance of the past as a standard of guidance, and on the other hand total repudiation of that past; or is there not still another alternative which will harmonize the present with the past, individualism with authority, liberty with law? I think there is this alternative, and it seems to me that the true course to follow is to try to gather the spirit and reason for the specific observances of the early Church, and then having discerned the principles underlying these usages, to endeavor to apply them with the necessary modifications to modern Church life, social life, and the individual life. We should be neither wilful and obstinate iconoclasts, neither should we be blind worshippers of tradition. We must remember that reasons and principles lay back of most of the Lenten rules which the early Church laid down, and if we can grasp them, then I think we shall have a clue for our present conduct.

Now what are the principles lying back of the details of Lenten observance? Are they not that there is a moral necessity in the life of every individual to give at stated times, in addition to the ordinary regular attention to the religious life, some special attention to religious duties, to the stirring up and quickening of the spiritual life to increased piety and devotion; also the need of there being some fixed time set for this special attention to be given, otherwise the weakness of our nature will not of itself make the time; and also that this set time is intended for us to get at the

roots of our religious life, " to dig about them
and dung them "; to set before ourselves the
duty of earnest and sincere self-examination,
of true repentance, of steady self-discipline;
and to achieve these the Church would afford
us increased services as helps, multiplied sermons and communions; and also because she
knows that we are easily distracted she would
suggest the inexpediency at this time of Lent
of engaging in festivities, pleasures, banquet-
ings—perfectly lawful and harmless in themselves in moderation, but which at this season would perhaps seriously interfere with our
attention and determined efforts to win and
maintain a higher level of holy thought and
life.

This then is, I think, the position of the
Church to-day: It recognizes the changed
conditions of thought and life, and how impossible it is to prescribe details of conduct,
and to regulate the minutiæ of domestic life.
She knows, too, that with the greatest diversity
of circumstances to prescribe minute details

and rules for conduct would be likely to injure
some where it was intended to help; and
perhaps still more it might lead some to a
certain unconscious reliance upon the meritori-
ousness of works, supposing that outward
observances made up for inward reform—a
mistake that all too minute regulation of life is
apt to engender;—that formality is necessarily
sincerity, and that the postures of the body indicate the posture of the heart: accordingly
the Church would lay down broad principles
such as I have already stated and leave them
for each of us to apply to our individual circumstances. She says now is the holy season
of Lent—called so because of its purpose, *viz*.
to increase in us holiness—a time it is for self-
examination and prayer, a time for self-discipline and charity, a time for repentance and forgiveness, a time to draw closer to God and to
realize more truly the sweetness of communion with Him, a time to consider how
transitory this life is and how we are hastening
to the life beyond the veil;—therefore increased

services are afforded which may be helpful if you will use them as helps, but the Church does not say how many services or which you shall attend, she leaves that to you to decide according to your individual circumstances. Once more, she advises self-denial and abstinence, but she does not prescribe the precise form it shall take, she leaves that to you to decide. If you are lovers of rich living, then it might take the form of abstinence from food or luxuries of diet; if you are excessively fond of gaiety and pleasure and of social enjoyment, then your abstinence might take the form of seclusion, retirement, the abandonment of pleasures which so fritter away what holy thought and purpose you possess; if you are fond of gay clothing, then your abstinence might take the form of dressing in less striking costumes; if you are fond of hoarding, then your abstinence might take the form of almsgiving in more generous and bountiful measure; if your tongue is given easily to slander or to speak harshly, then your absti.

nence might take the form of learning to speak well and kindly of your neighbor. Thus without multiplying illustrations, we may each apply the principles which lie at the bottom for the appointment of this holy season to every relation of our life, ecclesiastical, civil, and domestic; yes, if we will, we may apply these principles with even greater minuteness than the early Church ever could, because of the great subdivision of life which obtains to-day, and so by the diversity of application to differing individual needs and circumstances we can each of us make this season more searching and more helpful than any arbitrary imposition of specific rules common to all alike.

This then is the thought I would close with. Circumstances to-day differ radically from what they did in the early post-Nicene age. The thought and life of our time are also totally different, yet in spite of changed circumstances our deepest needs are the same, and our human nature with its weakness and follies, its crimes and its sins is the same. The fundamental principles governing the spiritual life remain to-day as true as they did 1500 years ago. We need some set time for special examination and prayer, and determined effort to overcome besetting sins and rise to the life of righteousness, but different conditions of life require different application of the means at our disposal. Individual prescription must take the place of ecclesiastical prescription ; only in the broad liberty granted to us of personal application let us beware lest our very liberty tempt us to make no application whatsoever, and thus we lose not only what benefit individual prescription but also what benefit external prescription might afford us. Let not our liberty run to license. Let not the boast of possessing principles lead us to ignore all practice. The season of Lent is yours to profit withal—see that you do not fail of profit because the Church has not prescribed minute rules to govern your conduct and life, has not imposed upon you the tithe of mint, anise and cummin.

IV.

FASTING.

IV.

FASTING.

He that eateth, eateth to the Lord, for he giveth God thanks; and he that eateth not, to the Lord he eateth not, and giveth God thanks. *Romans* xiv. 6.

THE question of fasting is one that has always given more or less occasion of difference of opinion, both as to its necessity, and also as to its practice. By some fasting has been looked upon as an end in itself, and a rigid observance has been insisted upon; by others it has been looked upon only as a means to an end and so modifications have been made according to circumstances; by others again its value either as end or means is absolutely denied and never practiced. Until the end of time there will doubtless be these differences of views dependent on the temperament or religious associations of individuals.

Still it may be stated that the practice of
fasting is by no means limited to Christians.
Fasting is common among many Oriental relig-
ionists, and indeed we may say that the ascetic
idea of the value of the mortification of the
flesh by fasting or other bodily discipline is
Oriental rather than Occidental.   To this very
day among Eastern nations, some of the forms
of religion of the East put a high value on
fasting, and see in it either a means of attain-
ing a high state of sanctity or else regard it as
an end in itself.   Even Islam has its annual
monthly fast of Ramadan, which is kept by
Mohammedans with religious strictness.

In considering the question of fasting in the
Christian Church and its relation to the Lenten
season, I shall not enter into any abstract dis-
cussion of the value or non-value of fasting, but
simply endeavor to state what was the actual
practice in the early Church, and note certain
consequences of abuse which followed upon
the attempt to lay down minute rules for fasting.   When we approach this subject we need

to bear in mind the early geographical origin
of the Church, *viz.* its origin in Eastern lands
and among an Eastern people. We must
remember the associations, the atmosphere of
thought, the native practices and habits which
environed the early Christians, if we are to
gain a fair estimate of their regard for fasting.
Let us remember then that the teachers and
converts of the early Church were chiefly
Orientals, whose manner of life was totally
different from ours; let us also consider that
the difference of climate between the East and
the West must never be lost sight of. With
these preliminary thoughts we may now proceed to consider the usages of fasting during
Lent in the early Church.

I. *Time.* Daily—how long? Weekly—
how many days? The first fact that we note
concerning fasting particularly in the Eastern
Church is the strictness with which the fast
was observed. It "consisted in a perfect
abstinence from all sustenance for the whole
day till evening" in the case of those who

were piously disposed and able to abstain thus long. Others "fasted till nine o'clock, that is three in the afternoon." In regard to the days of the week, the Eastern Church kept as fast days all days of Lent except Saturday and Sunday; while the Western Church kept Saturday as well. This accounts for the difference of time of beginning the Lenten fast which exists between the Eastern and Western Churches, though the actual days of fasting agree in number. There were also certain special usages in connection with fasting that were limited more to the week before Easter, such as absolute fasting for the whole week if possible by those able to forego food entirely for so long a time, or the disuse of food by others through the days of Good Friday and Easter-even. But apart from these more rigorous practices we may say that fasting in the early Church meant a total abstinence from food on all the strict fasting days of Lent until three in the afternoon, or even until the evening.

II. *Kind and variety of food, also its quality.* We next ask what was the practice as to the food to be taken, after fasting, because this is a point on which much misapprehension exists to-day by reason of the modern usage of the Roman church. In this respect of the kind of food to be taken, we learn that in the early Church a great variety, in fact all varieties of food were allowed. The historian Socrates, writing of the diverse practices of the early Church in regard to its Lenten fast, says, "Some abstained from all living creatures; others of all living creatures only ate fish; some ate fowls together with fish; others abstained from berries and eggs; others ate dry bread only; and some not so much as that." In this account we notice the wide latitude of choice, there being no restriction in kinds of food. The great object was to practice moderation in eating, was to put a restraint upon excessive indulgence. We may safely say that in the beginning there was no rule requiring abstinence during Lent from any special kinds

of food, whether flesh, fowl, or otherwise, provided after the period of abstinence had ex-
pired all foods were used with sobriety and in
moderation. The abstinence and fast consisted therefore not in abstaining from any
particular kind of food, but in moderate use of
all foods. Generally, indeed, there was abstinence from " flesh and wine and fish and all
other delicacies at this season ; but yet there
was no such universal rule, or custom, in this
matter, but that when men had fasted all the
day, they were allowed to refresh themselves
with a moderate supper upon flesh or any
other food without distinction." So soon
however as restrictions in kinds of food were
attempted, straightway the ingenuity of man
found means of observing the letter yet of
violating its spirit. "The greatest ascetics
made no scruple to eat flesh in Lent when a
just occasion required it," but there were
some observers of Lent who made a pretence
of fasting because they abstained from flesh
meat, while they deliberately violated the

spirit of abstinence. St. Augustine has a word for these self-deceivers. " There are some observers of Lent," says he, "that study deliciousness more than religion, and seek out new pleasures for the belly, more than how to chastise the concupiscence of the old man. . . . They are afraid of any vessels in which flesh has been boiled, as if they were unclean; and yet in their own flesh fear not the luxury of the throat and the belly. These men fast, not to diminish their wonted voracity by temperance, but by deferring a meal to increase their immoderate greediness. For when the time of refreshment comes they rush to their plentiful tables as beasts to their manger, and stuff their bellies with great variety of artificial and strange sauces, taking in more by devouring than they are able to digest again by fasting. There are some, likewise, who drink no wine, that they may provide themselves other more agreeable liquors to gratify their taste, rather than set forward their salvation; as if Lent were intended not for the observation of a pious humiliation, but as an occasion of seeking out new pleasures." Thus we see that as soon as men were limited to particular kinds of food the principle of abstinence was violated, though the letter might be kept. St. Augustine on this violation of the spirit of abstinence says not unjustly that that was no fast if the " abstinence of the day was spoiled by any immoderate indulgence of an evening banquet; much less did he esteem it a fast to dine upon delicacies as a substitute for the abstinence from flesh."

The early Church did not make the fast consist in simple abstinence from a particular kind of food; it would reach a deeper principle and result than such superficial prescription. " The pretence of keeping Lent only by change of diet from flesh to fish, or a more delicious food, which allows men the use of wine and other delicacies, is but a mock fast, and a mere innovation utterly unknown to the ancients."

If I understand the principle of fasting

which the early Church laid down, it would be
that fasting consisted not simply in abstinence
from food for a stated length of time, and
from a certain kind of food, but it was the practice of moderation in all kinds of food at all
times, with a total abstinence from food for a
certain portion of all the fasting days of Lent;
and that together with his moderation should
be exercised charity, almsgiving, forgiveness,
and other Christian deeds of mercy. We also
are led to believe that the liberty of the individual was left untouched in great measure;
that each was to be his own judge of his
ability to fast.   In proof of this we may quote
from the greatest of the early preachers, and
also most reasonable of Fathers, St. Chrysostom.   He says to his hearers during Lent,
"If thou canst not pass all the day fasting by
reason of bodily weakness no wise man can
condemn thee for this. For we have a kind
and merciful Lord, who requires nothing of us
above our strength. He neither requires abstinence from meat, nor fasting simply of us;

nor that for this end, we should continue without eating only; but that sequestering ourselves from worldly affairs, we should spend
all our leisure time in spiritual things. For if
we would order our lives soberly, and lay out
our spare hours upon spiritual things, and eat
only so much as we had need of and nature
required, and spend our whole lives in good
works, we should not need the help of fasting."
Then he proceeds to advise as follows—at-
tempting thereby to correct abuses in the
matter which had become prevalent: "If
therefore there be any here present who are
hindered by bodily infirmity and cannot continue all the day fasting, I exhort them to have
regard to the weakness of their bodies. . . .
For there are many ways besides abstinence
from meat which will open to us the door of
confidence towards God. He therefore that
eats and cannot fast, let him give the more
plentiful alms; let him be more fervent in
his prayers; let him show the greater alacrity
and readiness in hearing the divine oracle; let

him be reconciled to his enemies, and forget injuries, and cast all thoughts of revenge out of his mind. He that does these things will show forth the true fasting which the Lord chiefly requires."

Thus we see it was something more than abstinence in eating and drinking that was involved in the Lenten fast as St. Chrysostom understood it. "Tell them what the apostle says, 'Both he that eateth, eateth to the Lord ; and he that eateth not, to the Lord he eateth not, and giveth God thanks,' therefore he that fasteth giveth God thanks, who has enabled him to bear the labor of fasting; and he that eateth gives God thanks likewise, that this is no prejudice to the salvation of his soul if he be otherwise willing and obedient." In a word, every particular church in the beginning in a great measure on this question of fasting "left all her members to judge of their own abilities by Christian prudence and discretion ; exhorting men to fast, but imposing rigidly upon none more than they were able and willing to

bear, nor enforcing it under pain of ecclesiastical censure."

Our study so far will lead us to learn that
fasting was not an end in itself. It had two
objects—one which looked to some gain for
the individual practicing it; another which
looked to procuring some benefit for others.
For the individual profit it was desired that
the one fasting should practice moderation,
that he devote more time to spiritual exercises, that he abstain from unseemly and un-
seasonable amusements and from pleasures at
this time inexpedient. For the profit of
others it was desired that the faster should
exercise forgiveness, cast out revenge, and
through savings made from abstinence in food,
luxuries and other expenses, be enabled to
assist more liberally with alms the poor.
Thus one of the early Fathers says, "That which
is gained by the fast at dinner ought not to
be turned into a feast at supper but expended
for the feeding of the poor." So too Leo the
Great :—" That which is not expended upon

our tables should be laid out in alms, and then it will bring us in great gain." So Chrysologus: "Fasting without mercy is but an image of famine; fasting without works of piety is only an occasion of covetousness, because by such sparing what is taken from the body only swells in the purse."

Herein lies the danger of all bodily and outward observances that they become formal, that they produce no spiritual profit, unless we guard our motives, and constantly examine ourselves.

Even in so early a time as that of St. Chrysostom the danger was noticed; already the abuse of fasting was making way. He says, "It was usual in Lent for the people to ask one another how many weeks they had fasted, and one would answer he had fasted two weeks, another three, another all." To this that Father replies: "And what advantage is it, if we have kept the fast without mending our morals? If another says 'I have fasted the whole Lent,' say thou 'I had an enemy and I am reconciled to him; I had a custom of reviling and I have left it off; I was used to swearing and I have broken the evil habit.' It is of no advantage to fast, if our fasting do not produce such fruits as these." "Let no one," he continues, "place his confidence in fasting only, if he continues in his sins without reforming. For it may be, that one who fasts not at all may obtain pardon, if he has the excuse of bodily infirmity; but he that does not correct his sins can have no excuse." And once more, to correct the abuse of supposing that a bare fast was sufficient, St. Chrysostom warns, "Let us set a guard upon our ears, our tongues, our minds, and not think that bare fasting till the evening is sufficient for our salvation. What profit is it to fast and eat nothing all the day if you give yourself to playing at dice, and other vain pastimes, and spend the whole day many times in perjuries and blasphemies? The true fast is abstinence from vices. He that fasts ought above all things to bridle his anger; to learn meekness and clemency; to have a contrite heart; to banish the thoughts of all inordinate desires; to set the watchful eye of God before his eyes, and His uncorrupted judgment; to set himself above riches, and exercise great liberality in giving of alms; and to expel every evil thought against his neighbor out of his soul. This is the true fast. Therefore let this be our care and let us not imagine as many do, that we have fasted rightly when we have abstained from eating until evening. This is not the thing required of us, but that together with our abstinence from meat, we should abstain from those things that hurt the soul, and diligently exercise ourselves in things of a spiritual nature."

We are now in a position to gather up in a few sentences what was the fast of the early Church. We may say that if people were in health and able to endure fasting the rule and custom was that they should fast all the days of Lent—Saturday and Sunday excepted in the East, whereas in the West Saturday was

included. Next, that this fasting when practiced consisted in abstaining from food from
the morning until three in the afternoon, or
sometimes until the evening; further, that
originally there was no rule as to diet, but each
person decided for himself what the food
should be which he would eat after fasting,
taking care however that the repast after the
diurnal fast should be moderate, and that
abstinence from any particular kind of food
should not be made an excuse for indulging
immoderately in other foods even more delicious simply because they might not be flesh.
Next, as to the purpose of fasting, it was not an
end but a means; it looked to the spiritual
improvement of the faster, and also to the
temporal improvement of those less favored.
Fasting was designed for the individual to subdue his appetites, passions, anger, to increase
the life of the spirit, to raise the whole tone of
living; and next, designed for the benefit of
others, that by the repression of luxuries,
indulgences and expenses, the one thus prac-

ticing self-denial might bestow alms of all that was thus saved. What was saved was not to be kept for future indulgence, but was to be given to the poor, otherwise there was no virtue in economy and retrenchment. Then there were exceptions. In fact, every one decided for himself how rigid should be his fast, and for those unable to fast at all, the Church made ample allowance, insisting more on the need of spiritual fasting and discipline than on the physical, and so would put a check on those who might be inclined to indulge in the pharisaic complacency that their abstinence made them better than those who did not fast. This thought leads us to notice that the abuse of the purpose of fasting soon crept into the Church ; that by some the letter which kills was observed, whereas the spirit which giveth life was ignored.

But now we ask how shall we apply this practice of fasting to our modern church life, and to ourselves in this new continent unknown to the early Church. There will be no difficulty in seeing how far the practice can be adopted, if we keep in mind what one of the greatest of the Fathers of the early Church would insist upon, *viz.* that fasting was a means to an end, not the end. If, therefore, as a means it fails to be valuable, then of course it is to be disused. We must consider whether it does fail in our time and land to be useful, or whether it can be practiced so as to benefit us.

I am of the opinion that no definite rule for fasting can be laid down, and the practice even when adopted can only be observed with the largest allowances and exceptions owing to differences of climate, labor, living and individuals. Those who live in cold regions need more food, and more frequently, in order to sustain life, than those do who live in warm latitudes. Again, those who work hard, as most do in our land, need to eat more than those who labor intermittently, as in Eastern lands. Once more, those who eat less at each meal will need to eat oftener than those whose habitual practice is to eat only two meals a day, but then to eat fully. Let me here quote the words of one who would press the duty of physical fasting as far as it can be. "The Church of England," says Blunt, "has not expressly defined any rule on the subject of fasting" (still less has our American Church). "The work that is set before most persons, in the Providence of God, at the present day, makes it quite impossible for those who have to do it, to fast every day for six weeks until evening, or even to take one meal only in the day. And the ordinary mode of living is so restrained among religious persons, that such a custom would soon reduce them to an invalid condition, in which they could not do their duty properly in the station of life to which God has called them, whether in the world or in the sanctuary. And although it may seem at first that men ought to be able to fast in the nineteenth century as strictly as they did in the sixteenth, the twelth or the third, yet it should be remembered that (our) continuous labor of life was unknown to the great majority

of persons in ancient days; and (also) that the
quantity and quality of the food which now
forms a full meal is only equivalent to what
would have been an extremely spare one until
comparatively modern days." "The problem
the modern Christian has to solve is to recon-
cile the duty of fasting. . . . with the duty of
properly accomplishing the work which God
has set him to do, that he may fulfil both duties
as a faithful servant." Once more, because of
our large differences of occupation, manner of
life, habits, no one can lay down for another
what shall be the degree of abstinence which
he shall observe. Yet because no one can lay
down for me, nor I for you what degree of
abstinence shall be practiced, shall there be
no abstinence ? There will be if we keep in
mind the purpose of abstinence, though the
form it may take will not necessarily always
be physical fasting. Thus those who already
are inclined to gluttony might well practice
fasting ; those who are epicurean in their
tastes, and are desirous of rich living and

delicacies, might forego some of this choice living ; while those who without temptations of the palate are tempted by gaiety, pleasures, social intercourse, might abstain from " theatres, balls, parties, sumptuous costumes." These several forms of abstinence given as illustrations —they are as manifold as the habits and occupations of men—will have their advantage in being just the forms of discipline needed for our differing temptations by giving us what we have saved in money for enlarged almsgiving, what we have saved in time for increased attendance at the public services in church, or for private devotions.

And now after what has been said, we might well ask is there much of the fasting of the early Church practiced by us—the actual abstinence from food throughout the day? I venture to think there is not ; and I think that the whole manner of our modern life precludes the ability or the need.

What then is the thought and practical lesson to be gained ? Is it not to realize the end or purpose of all the early Church observances of fasting, to realize that "the honor of fasting," as St. Chrysostom says, "consists not in abstinence from food, but in withdrawing from sinful practices. For let not the mouth only fast but also the eye, and the ear, and the feet, and the hands, and all the members of our bodies. Let the hands fast by being pure from rapine and avarice. Let the feet fast by ceasing to run to unlawful spectacles. Let the eyes fast, being taught never to fix themselves rudely upon handsome countenances, or to busy themselves with strange beauties. Let the ear fast, refusing to receive evil speakings and calumnies. Let the mouth, too, fast from disgraceful speeches and railing. For what doth it profit if we abstain from birds and fishes; and yet bite and devour our brethren?" In a word, "what advantage shall we gain by abstinence from meats, if we do not also expel the evil habits of the soul?"

The end of all abstinence is self-discipline in its widest sense of body, mind and will. If you can practice fasting, brethren, do so, if it will chasten your bodies and bring them into subjection, but see to it that you fast not simply to say you have so done. If it be not a means to a higher end—if fasting tend only to self-righteousness, then I say even as did Chrysostom of old, of what use fasting if the soul be not purified?

We may sum up the matter for ourselves somewhat as follows: Fasting is but a subordinate practice—a special application—of the higher and wider principle of abstinence. Abstinence is for all, fasting may be only for some. Its object is not to subdue the flesh, but to subdue the flesh to the spirit. As an end in itself it is valueless; as a means to an end it may be most valuable. Do not let us talk about it as a rule of the Church and then pay no heed to it. The Church to-day as in its earliest days, would lay down the principle of abstinence in its highest and widest sense, and leave the application of this principle to each individual to make according to his time and circumstances. And when all has been said, it may be well to remember the words of the apostle: "He that eateth eateth to the Lord, for he giveth God thanks ; and he that eateth not to the Lord he eateth not and giveth God thanks." And lest we who may practice fasting condemn those who fast not let us further remember the apostolic precept: "Who art thou that judgest another man's servant? To his own master he standeth or falleth."

V.

HOLY WEEK.

V.

HOLY WEEK.

Now the feast of unleavened bread drew nigh, which is called the Passover. *Luke* xxii. i.

IN our consideration of the early origin of Lent, its purpose and its practices, we had to omit mention of some of the usages because of their special connection with a certain portion of the Lenten season. To-day we are in a position to take up the observances connected with the Great Week, as it was called —the week before Easter. In later times and in our time the week before Easter is known as Holy Week; but in the early Church—and it is the customs and usages of the early rather than the later or mediæval Church which we have been considering—in the early Church

this week was called the "*hebdomas magna*" or
the "great week" before Easter.

And first it was so called as St. Chrysostom
tells us, "not because it consisted of longer
days, or more in number than other weeks, but
because at this time great things were wrought
for us by our Lord. For in this week the
ancient tyranny of the devil was dissolved,
death was extinct, the strong man was bound,
his goods were spoiled, sin was abolished, the
curse was destroyed, Paradise was opened,
heaven became accessible, men and angels
were joined together, the middle wall of parti-
tion was broken down, the barriers were taken
out of the way, the God of Peace made peace
between things in heaven and things on earth,
therefore it is called 'the great week.'" Because then of the great honor and special reverence in which it was held, special observances
were connected with it, and still more with
certain days of this week.

We will consider the observances first for
the week in general, and next for certain of the
days in particular.

I. (*a*) This week was the culmination of the season of Lent, therefore at this time many increased their labors and disciplined themselves with greater strictness than ever. Thus in the matter of fasting, "whereas in the foregoing part of Lent, some refreshment was taken every evening, and the Sabbath (*i. e.* Saturday) was never observed as a fast, now many not only fasted on the Sabbath in this week, but added to it, some one day, some two, some three, some four, some five days, which they passed in perfect abstinence, eating nothing all this week till the morning of the resurrection."

(*b*) Then again, in the matter of almsgiving and charity, during this week many gave more liberal alms, and "exercised all kinds of charity to those who stood in need of it. For the nearer they approached to the passion and resurrection of Christ by which all the blessings in the world were poured forth upon men, the more they thought themselves obliged to show all manner of acts of mercy and kindness toward their brethren." St. Chrysostom says

of this week, "As the Jews went forth to meet
Christ when He had raised Lazarus from the
dead, so now not one city, but all the world go
forth to meet him, not with palm branches in
their hands, but with alms-deeds, humanity,
virtue, fasting, tears, prayers, watchings, and all
kinds of piety which they offer to Christ their
Lord."

(*c*) Once more, in the domestic economy of
families, "this week before Easter, and the following week was a time of rest and liberty to
servants. All servants had a vacation from
their ordinary bodily labor, that they might
have more leisure and opportunity to attend
the worship of God and concerns of their
soul." And to give even more effect to this
practice than simple good will there was a rule
directing, "In the whole 'great week' (before
Easter) and the week following, let servants
rest from their labors; because the one is the
time of our Lord's passion, and the other of
His resurrection; and servants have need to be
instructed in the knowledge of those mysteries."

(*d*) Again, as many servants were also slaves, this week was the time when many masters in great charity granted freedom to their slaves, "in imitation of the spiritual liberty which Christ, at this time, had procured for all mankind."

(*e*) Civil government was also affected after the alliance of the State with the Church. During this week civil business ceased, and courts were closed. Referring to this great week St. Chrysostom says, "And not only we, but the emperors of the world honor this week, making it a time of vacation from all civil business; that the magistrates, being at liberty from business of the law, may spend all these days in spiritual services. Let the doors of the courts, say they, now be shut up; let all disputes and all kinds of contention and punishment cease; let the executioner's hands rest a little; common blessings are wrought for us all by our common Lord, let some good be done by us His servants." This cessation from all business of the law was decreed

by Constantine, the design being "that nothing of animosity, or contention, or cruelty, or
punishment, or bloodshed, should appear at
this holy season, when all men were laboring
to obtain mercy and pardon by the blood of
Christ; and that men sequestering themselves
from all civil and worldly business might with
greater assiduity attend the exercises of piety
which were peculiar to the solemn occasion."

(*f*) But imperial recognition of this solemn
season did not end simply with the closing of
courts.   Mercy was shown to prisoners.   "Imperial letters," says St. Chrysostom, "are sent
abroad at this time commanding all prisoners
to be set at liberty from their chains.   For as
our Lord, when He descended into hell, set
free those that were detained by death, so the
servants according to their power, imitating
the kindness of their Lord, loose men from
their corporal bonds when they have no power
to relax the spiritual."   This imperial indulgence was shown especially during this great
week by the Emperors to all prisoners—crim-

inals as well as debtors. We notice also that this indulgence was granted not only in the East but also in the West. For St Ambrose of Milan says, " The holy days of the last week in Lent, was the time when the bonds of debtors used to be loosed." Pardon was granted " to all criminals who lay bound in prison for their faults, except some that were of a more malignant and unpardonable nature."

Such then were some of the special observ- 7 ances of this great week—ecclesiastical, domestic, civil. Greater strictness, more rigorous fasting, deeper and prolonged devotion, larger almsgiving, increased deeds of charity and works of mercy, servants were given time to attend the services of the church and to be instructed, slaves were often given their freedom, the courts were closed, legal business ceased, and even prisoners—criminals and debtors—with the exception of malignant and capital prisoners were pardoned and set free in these solemn days of the great week preceding Easter.

II. (*a*) We pass on now to consider observances connected with certain days of this great week. The first of these is Thursday. This day has had many names derived from some circumstance connected with the first great Thursday, but many of them are of late origin. Thus we have the names—the day of the Supper of the Lord ; the birthday of the Eucharist ; the birthday of the cup ; the day of the mysteries ; the day of the feet-washing, and Maundy Thursday. Most of these names explain themselves except perhaps the last. " Maundy Thursday is in all probability a vernacular corruption in English of ' Dies Mandati ' *i. e.*, the day of the commandment, because on this day our Saviour washed his disciples' feet, and gave them commandment to follow His example ; or because He instituted the Sacrament of His Supper upon this day, commanding His disciples to do the same in remembrance of Him." The name, however, which is most frequently used in the early Eastern Church is that used by St. Chrysostom, *viz.* " the holy and great fifth day."

(*b*) Having considered the names we may now proceed to consider some of the special observances of this holy and great fifth day—called by us Maundy Thursday, Thursday before Easter, or Thursday in Holy Week.

There are two acts of our Lord on the Thursday of the first holy week which are constantly called to our mind by the evangelical records, *viz.* the feet-washing, and the institution of the Last Supper. As to the feet-washing, this custom has been preserved in various forms, and for various periods by some branches of the Church. Its connection in the early Church, however, was chiefly with baptism. Its perpetual obligation was never universally acknowledged. Says Origen : " It is not necessary for any one who wishes to obey all the commandments of Jesus, literally to perform the act of feet-washing." Once again, in answer to a set of questions, concerning ecclesiastical usages and the different customs in different parts of the Church, put to him by a friend, St. Augustine replies, " As to the feet-washing, since the Lord recommended this because of its being an example of that humility which He came to teach, as He Himself afterwards explained, the question has arisen at what time it is best, by literal performance of this work, to give public instruction in the important duty (*i. e.*, humility) which it illustrates, and this time (of Lent) was suggested in order that the lesson taught by it might make a deeper and more serious impression. Many, however, have not accepted this as a custom, lest it should be thought to belong to the ordinance of Baptism ; and some have not hesitated to deny it any place among our ceremonies." We may perhaps accept what a wise commentator—Alford—remarks, that "the custom of literally and ceremonially washing the feet in obedience to this commandment is not found before the fourth century." Since then it has been adopted for a time in parts of the Church, and Maundy Thursday has been the day set apart for the fulfilment of this command. The present Bishop of Durham in his commentary on St. John's Gospel sums up the practice historically by saying, "By a decree of the XVIIIth Council of Toledo, 694, it (*i. e.,* feet-washing) was made obligatory on the Thursday in Holy Week 'throughout the churches of Spain and Gaul.' The practice was continued in England by English sovereigns till the reign of James II.; and as late as 1731 the Lord High Almoner washed the feet of the recipients of the royal gifts at Whitehall on Maundy Thursday." Even to this day, though the feet-washing is discontinued, there is still in use in the Chapel Royal at Whitehall an "office for the Royal Maundy," where on Maundy Thursday there are distributed gifts of money and clothing to a certain number of poor men and women, and during the distribution the bishop who acts as the Queen's Almoner, and his assistant are girded with long linen towels. The custom of the feet-washing is still retained at St. Peter's, Rome, and the practice is also maintained by certain Christian sects such as the Mennonites, and

until recently by the United Brethren. The
literal practice and its obligation we have seen
were not required as a universal custom in the
early Church, nor indeed was it made a matter
of church appointment in any churches until
the seventh century in those of Gaul and
Spain.

(*c*) .Let us now pass on to consider the
second act of our Lord on the Thursday before
His crucifixion, *viz.* that of the institution of
the Last Supper. It had become the custom
quite early in the history of the Christian
Church to celebrate the Lord's Supper in the
morning—a custom at first due more perhaps
to political exigencies than to any doctrinal
significance—but on this great fifth day "in
some of the Latin churches, the communion
was administered in the evening after supper,
in imitation of the communion of the apostles
at our Lord's last supper." In some places
St. Augustine tells us the communion "was
administered twice on this day; in the morning for the sake of such as could not keep the

day a fast; and in the evening for those that fasted till evening, when they ended their fast and received the communion after supper." Thus we see that though custom had caused the celebration of the communion to take place in the morning, there were exceptions to the rule, and the great exception was on this Maundy Thursday evening. We know the strong objections to evening communion in our Church, and yet if to-day in any of our parish churches this practice should be maintained according to the liberty and also prevalent practice of the early Church, it would ill become us to criticise or condemn those who so desire on this day to commemorate in the evening the first institution of this sacrament. Certainly the precedent and practice of the primitive Church would countenance the custom. There are some weighty words on this subject in a recently published book of the Bishop of Manchester.

(*d*) Again, this great Thursday was marked by other usages. On this day the candidates

for baptism "publicly rehearsed the creed before the Bishop or Presbyter in the church,"
and until the close of the fifth or the beginning
of the sixth century this was the only occasion in the year when the creed was openly
recited.   It was not until the close of the fifth
or the beginning of the sixth century that it
became the practice to regularly recite the
Nicene Creed in the Communion Office, at
which time it was introduced according to
some authorities by Peter the Fuller, the intru-
ding patriarch of Antioch ; according to other
authorities by Timothy, Bishop of Constantinople.   And singularly both these bishops are
charged with being Monophysites.

(*e*) Again, this great Thursday was the day
set apart for the solemn ablutions of the candidates for baptism on Easter-even.   St. Augustine replying to some questions on this custom
says, " If you ask me whence originated the
custom of using the bath on (this) day, nothing
occurs to me when I think of it as more likely
than that it was to avoid the offence to decency

which must have been given at the Baptismal font, if the bodies of those to whom that rite was to be administered were not washed on some preceding day from the uncleanness consequent upon their strict abstinence from ablutions during Lent." It was also the practice with many who had already been baptized, to abstain from bathing through Lent, thinking they thereby practiced greater self-discipline, and they too took this day as the day for ending this form of abstinence by bathing.

(*f*) Once more, the great fifth day—though some defer the matter until the following day —was the day on which penitents were absolved or reconciled. "All the doors (of the church) were thrown open to intimate that penitent offenders, whether they came from the East or from the West, from the North or from the South, or from whatever quarter of the world, would be received into the bosom of the Church, and into the arms of divine mercy."

(*g*) Also "on this day it was customary for servants to receive the communion."

There are still the usages of Good Friday, and the great Sabbath or Easter-even to be considered, but these we will postpone to the next address.

In conclusion I would remark that of the customs we have considered some have disappeared and been discontinued because they were of temporary value; some have been retained because of their permanent worth. What we need to remember at this day is that usages arose according to needs and circumstances, that when these needs ceased naturally the usages ceased. Again, we must notice that the usages we have considered prevailed chiefly in the East, and in the undivided Church. But to-day we live under different conditions and circumstances, and our aim should be not to imitate in any particular the usage of the ancient Church, a practice perhaps established to meet a certain temporary need, or passing phase of thought; but to endeavor to separate the essential from the non-essential, and maintaining the same principles and spirit of the

Lenten season which prevailed in early days, to apply that spirit and those principles under necessary modifications and if necessary entirely different usages, to our modern needs and circumstances. We notice plainly that owing to our changed modes of life, many of the ancient usages would to-day find no room for exercise, no point of contact in our life. The practice of feet-washing had a certain significance in the East, where ceremonial ablutions were of such consequence, and perhaps the practice even to-day in the Orient might be maintained with advantage ; but in the West, where the practice had become so formal and stiffened with ceremonial, the principle it was designed to inculcate, *viz.* humility, may perhaps best be practiced by disregarding rather than observing the custom. The practice of humility may well find expression in some other rite more applicable to and needed for our times and life. So again the practice of the ablution of the catechumens on this day has ceased to have any value in the West, because not only is infant baptism more extensively practiced, but also the custom of deferring baptism until Easter has largely passed away; and the further belief that abstinence from bathing is a mark of self-discipline or a means to the attainment of a higher state of sanctity has now little credence or reception among Christians, who believe that "cleanliness is next to godliness," a phrase often supposed by some to be of scriptural authority.

In the face of diversity of usage and of opinion as to the value of the retention or disuse of certain customs and observances of the early Church in the present day, no word seems to me more fitting to recall and act upon than that written now nearly 1300 years ago by Gregory the Great, Bishop of Rome, to Augustine, monk and first Archbishop of Canterbury, concerning this very Anglican Church of which we are members. Augustine on his arrival in England found that though the Saxons and Angles were heathen, yet there was in existence a British Church. But its customs differed in many respects from those to which Augustine, the monk of Rome, was accustomed. Accordingly he writes to Gregory for counsel and advice, and that large and wise minded man—however we may differ in regard to his ambitious designs—wrote back to Augustine : "You, my brother, are acquainted with the customs of the Roman Church, in which you were brought up. But it is my pleasure that if you have found anything either in the Roman, or the Gallican, or any other Church which may be more acceptable to Almighty God, you carefully make choice of the same ; and sedulously teach the Church of the English [*i. e.* the Church of the Saxons and Angles, not the British Church] which is at present new in the faith, whatsoever you can gather from the several Churches. For things are not to be loved for the sake of places, but places for the sake of good things. Select therefore from each Church those things that are pious, religious, and correct."

The same wise words are needed to-day.

Many would enforce one and only one usage or custom, forgetting that the practice of the primitive Church was to allow great diversity of customs; others again would object to all ancient usages, these also forgetting that unrestrained individual liberty most frequently degenerates unto lawless license. The true spirit is, I think, to accept as nearly as we can the customs and usages of the early Church which have been found universally applicable, *i. e.*, which are applicable to our unchanged needs as human beings in this remote land, and in these later years, and which the Church to-day has accepted and sanctioned ; but to forego without pain or complaint all those practices and minute rites and usages which from the nature of the case could only be local and temporary. If we accept the order and the customs of the Church in this loyal spirit, we shall grant that there may be room for great diversity of customs and usages in God's Church throughout all the world, and yet with all this variation we may maintain our belief in " one body and one spirit, one Lord, one faith, one baptism, one God and Father of all, who is above all, and through all, and in us all."

VI.

HOLY WEEK.

VI.

HOLY WEEK.

Now the feast of unleavened bread drew nigh, which is called the Passover. Luke xxii. 1.

AS in the Jewish Church the feast of the Passover which commemorated the great deliverance from Egypt was celebrated by special preparations, so too as we draw near to the commemoration of the great spiritual deliverance of mankind by the sacrifice of the Saviour on the cross, the Church has always made special preparation for that event, and has commemorated it in most solemn manner.

We have considered the general observances of the early Church in connection with Holy Week, and also the special observances connected with the great Thursday of this week, to-day we shall consider the special observances connected with the remaining two days therein, and close our Lenten studies with some general reflections on the use and the abuse of Lent.

I. First we will consider the names given to the Friday of Holy Week. There have been many names given to this day, the earliest being as was most natural connected with the Jewish Passover, and the event which occurred on this day. One of the earliest names therefore given to Friday in Holy Week is "the day of the preparation," or as some would translate "the day of the Passover," thus indicating the connection of the day of the atonement for the sins of the whole world with the Jewish Passover when Israel was redeemed out of Egyptian bondage. Others again, leaving out of sight the parallel to Jewish history, fastened their thoughts more on the actual event of the day in connection with our Lord's life and work, accordingly this Friday is also known as "the day of our Lord's passion," or "Passion day." "In early English times this

Friday was known as Long Friday, called so perhaps on account of the long fastings and offices they then used." But the name by which this Friday has now been best known for many centuries among English speaking Christians is " Good Friday," called so " from the blessed effects of our Saviour's sufferings, which are the ground of all our joy ; and from those unspeakable good things he hath purchased for us by his death." So much for the name.

From the earliest times Good Friday has been observed with great solemnity. " Indeed, this day was one of those two great days which all Christians in general thought themselves obliged strictly to observe." " Even those who kept no other Lent, religiously observed this day and the following."

It was a day too when fasting was strictly kept and a general attendance at divine service was practiced. Work also ceased on this day, except works of charity.

Again, on this day, according to some authori-

ties, and not on the day preceding, penitents
who "had completed their penance for one,
two, three years or more the Lent preceding,
were absolved." " Nor was it only particular
absolutions that were granted to public penitents on this day of the Passion, but a general
absolution or indulgence was proclaimed to all
the people observing the day with fastings,
prayers, and true contrition or compunction."
Yet in time laxity crept in, and some churches
omitted the observance of these strict acts of
devotion.   On this day of the Lord's passion,
"the church doors were shut up, and no divine
service performed."   This laxity had to be cor-
rected by ecclesiastical censure, and in Spain,
where this loss of piety and decadence of
spirituality was specially marked, a canon had
to be passed, requiring the opening of churches
for service on this day.   This canon was
passed about the seventh century.

We come now to consider a custom which
bears more closely upon our own practice, in
regard to the administration of the Holy Com-

munion on Good Friday. The custom largely prevails in our Church to omit the administration of the Holy Communion on Good Friday. Just why, it would puzzle many to say. One reason is, perhaps many of us think that this omission has always been the rule of the Church. But has it? If we are to credit the early Fathers we are led to believe that with them even on Good Friday there was no omission. As early as the days of Tertullian (*cir.* 145–220) we read that in the African Church —and this would in great measure involve the whole of Latin Christianity—" the Eucharist was received on Sundays, the fifty days between Easter and Pentecost which were but one continual festival, and all their stationary days, *i. e.* Wednesdays and Fridays in every week throughout the year." Tertullian says expressly of these Wednesdays and Fridays " that they were always observed with receiving the Eucharist." In the Eastern Church St. Basil also agrees with Tertullian in making these stationary days " days of communion," and as Saturday was also always a feast day in the Eastern Church it appears " that in many churches they had the Communion four times every week—on Wednesdays, Fridays, Saturdays and Sundays." Further, if we are to take literally and not rhetorically many of the passages from St. Chrysostom and St. Augustine we may well believe that the communion was administered every day in the year. I mention this fact not that I deem it necessary we should do exactly as did the primitive Church, nor that we should reproduce every practice and adopt every usage which then prevailed, but simply to show what was the actual custom and thereby pass to the consideration of the custom which to-day prevails so largely, if not wholly with us, of omitting the administration of the communion on Good Friday. If the omission is based as it is by some on the alleged practice of the primitive Church, the omission is erroneously based, because as I have shown, the writings of the Fathers of the early Church would lead us to believe that the Communion was not omitted on this day. It is well to be informed of this, that we may not erroneously attribute our usage to ancient practice ; and further, it would be well to remember that oftentimes when we are said to be following ancient usage, we are really departing from it.

Once more, in the early Latin Church the Sacramentary of Gregory clearly indicates that there was Communion on Good Friday. In fact, as a learned English divine—Blunt—says, Communion " on this day was the prevailing custom of the Church until the tenth century at least."

Again, if we are to be guided by the implicit teaching of the English Church, according to her formularies, and also according to our own, we would revive the Communion on Good Friday. We know how the appointment of a Collect, Epistle, and Gospel for any day has so often been construed to imply that the Church thereby presupposes a celebration on that day ; if this be a valid inference then we see how the appointment of Collects, Epistle, and Gospel for Good Friday would point to the intention of the English Church, and also our own.

Next, when we consider what the Communion implies, surely there can be no day of the year when the Communion could be or ought to be more fitly administered than on the day on which our redemption was wrought by the sacrifice on the cross, the offering up of the Body and Blood of Christ. It has, I say, become customary with us to omit the Communion on Good Friday, but if we do omit it, let us remember it is a late usage, not that of the primitive Church, and if we really desire to follow the ancient Church in all her practices, then we should most certainly restore this of a Communion on Good Friday. But as I have endeavored to show during this course of studies our aim is not to blindly imitate any special practice, but to reasonably adopt with the liberty we possess those principles and practices of the early Church which we can adopt and fit to

our needs and circumstances. With the liberty
wherewith Christ has made us free we are
privileged to exercise our judgment and base
our methods and practices largely on our experience and needs. If, therefore, to-day we
omit the Communion on Good Friday, we are
justified in so doing if we base our omission on
the possession of the privilege of a true branch
of God's Church to adopt its customs to its
times and needs; only when we do so let us
distinctly remember our present usage is not
that of the primitive Church.

II. (*a*) Let us now pass to the consideration
of the Saturday in Holy Week. We know it
by the name of Easter-even, but in the early
Church it was known as the "Great Sabbath."
Here let me add a word of caution to remind
you that in all early use of this word Sabbath,
the primitive Church always meant by it Saturday, and not Sunday as many Christians to-day
mean when they use the word. This great
Sabbath had many special observances connected with it, and necessarily so, as it was the

link, so to speak, between the days of Lent of austerity, fasting and humiliation, and Easter, which was the great day of thanksgiving. This Great Sabbath therefore bears a twofold aspect —one of humiliation and one of rejoicing. It looks back to the cross, and forward to the resurrection.

(*b*) Let us consider first what we may call its Lenten aspect. This was the only Saturday or Sabbath in the year that was observed as a fast by the Eastern Church, and also by some of the Westerns. The day was kept most solemnly. In the well-known Constitutions of the Holy Apostles we read, "Do ye who are able fast the day of the preparation [*i. e.* Good Friday] and the Sabbath day entirely, tasting nothing until the cock-crowing of the night: but if anyone is not able to join them both together [*i. e.* to fast both Good Friday and Saturday] at least let him observe the Sabbath day." Thus sacredly was this Sabbath observed throughout the Church, and the fast continued till cock-crowing on the morning of Easter, which was the supposed time of our Lord's resurrection.

(*c*) Again, it was the custom to pass this night of the "great" Sabbath as a vigil, or season of watch in the Church, "to perform all parts of divine service, psalmody, reading the scriptures, the law, the prophets and the gospels, praying and preaching." The reason given for this watching was twofold; "because on this night our Lord was raised to life again after His Passion; and next, because on the same night he was expected to return to receive the kingdom of the world." As St. Jerome says, "It was a tradition among the Jews, that Christ would come at midnight, as He did upon the Egyptians at the time of the Passover," and so he thinks the custom arose "not to dismiss the people on the Paschal vigil before midnight, expecting the coming of Christ, after which, presuming on security, they kept the day a festival."

(*d*) As to the more joyful aspect of this day, we learn that this vigil after the persecution of

Christians had ceased, and the State and Church had become allied, was kept with great pomp. Eusebius tells us that in the time of Constantine the emperor "set up lofty pillars of wax to burn as torches all over the city, and lamps burning in all places so that the night seemed to outshine the sun at noon-day." And Gregory Nazianzen speaks of this custom of setting up lamps and torches in churches and private houses as symbolical "forerunners of that great Light, the Sun of Righteousness, arising on the world on Easter day."

(*e*) Then there was one more special custom connected with this great Saturday, the last which we shall note. This was the great day and night for baptizing catechumens who had been prepared by instruction and discipline during the preceding days of Lent. It had become the custom in the early Church after the first century and a half to defer the baptism of catechumens. There were two leading reasons for this delay. One was "to give sufficient time to the Catechumens to prepare

them for baptism; the other to reform their
defection, when they happened to turn lapsers
or apostates before their baptism." We must
remember that to be a Christian in the first
three centuries of our era meant the possibility
of being, and the willingness to be at any time
tried, and persecuted, and put to death; thus
the early Church desired by a long test before
baptism to have some partial assurance that
the catechumens were sincere, and would if
need be suffer martyrdom for the faith. There
had therefore gradually sprung up the custom
of deferring baptism to certain seasons, and of
the three special times of Epiphany, Easter and
Pentecost, the great Sabbath before Easter
was the time most favored. We read of
thousands being baptized at this season, in fact
on one special occasion during the episcopal
rule of St. Chrysostom, we hear of about three
thousand being baptized on one great Sabbath
in Constantinople, notwithstanding the lawless-
ness and the assaults of the soldiery on the
churches on that day. Thus the catechumens

having been baptized on this day or night before Easter, "were made complete Christians,
and admitted to the Communion" on Easter
day.

I think we see a reason why the "great" Sabbath before Easter was the time most favored
for baptism. This was the time when the
Lord was in the tomb just before His resurrection, and from the earliest days of the apostles
baptism has been connected with the death
and resurrection of Christ. Thus St. Paul
writing to the Romans says, "Know ye not
that so many of us as were baptized into Jesus
Christ were baptized into His death? Therefore we are buried with Him by baptism into
death ; that like as Christ was raised up from
the dead by the glory of the Father, even so
we also should walk in newness of life. For
if we have been planted together in the likeness of His death, we shall be also in the
likeness of His resurrection." Once again,
writing to the Colossians he tells them that
they are "buried with Christ in baptism,

wherein also ye are risen with Him through the faith of the operation of God, who hath raised Him from the dead." Thus as baptism was typical of the death and resurrection of Christ, so naturally Christians desired to be baptized at the time when the Church specially commemorated those events in our Lord's life; and therefore what day could be more fitly adapted than that which came between His death and resurrection—the Great Sabbath following Good Friday and preceding Easter?

Here we bring our studies of this subject to a close. We have endeavored during these Sunday mornings in Lent to learn of the early origin of Lent, its purpose, customs and observances. I hope those of us who have carefully followed the subject will be better able than ever to give a reason for our keeping of Lent, its origin, and the origin of many of its observances.

III. And now to sum up for ourselves a few lessons from the study in which we have been engaged, we gather, I think, two leading thoughts: that in connection with Lent there are first, certain permanent abiding principles deep as our nature which we need to maintain and apply; and secondly, that connected with the observance of Lent in the early Church were customs and usages which could only be of a temporary character. They were accidental; that is, adapted to the time, place, circumstances, political and social conditions of the age. Some of these we are justified to-day in maintaining; some owing to our changed circumstances and needs we cannot maintain. The truth we need to learn is that the principle which underlies the appointment of a Lenten fast is of more importance than the garment of usage which has been wrapped about it. We need to consider and weigh more why the season was observed than how it was observed. This leads us to remember that there may be such a thing as the abuse as well as the use of Lent.

We will briefly consider the use of Lent, and thereby gather certain indications of its abuse.

The use of Lent may be regarded in two aspects: first, to the individual; and secondly, to the Church and to the world.

First, as to the individual. We learn the need and importance of some definite time for special self-examination, of deepening our spiritual life; and we need this season appointed for us by some external authority, else what can be done by us at any time, will most likely be done at no time. We need then some time formally set apart for us for special self-examination, and for deepening our spiritual life, and this is to be done in two ways: first, by a sense of sin, and secondly, by a realization of God's love. The sense of sin will lead to penitence, self-discipline, and more frequent supplication; the realization of God's love will lead to a more joyful spirit, a deeper thankfulness, and so practically to enlarged alms-giving, greater charity, a readier spirit of forgiveness, a delight in communion with God. The Church, therefore, has for both these ends appointed increased services whereby we may express our repentance and devotion; and for our joy appointed increased opportunities for alms-giving and deeds of mercy.

And—to be brief—in the next aspect as to the Church and the world. The Church as a whole, apart from the individual, needs a season of penitence and prayer, needs to bemoan its lukewarmness and worldliness, needs to draw deeper from the fountain of truth, needs to have its light burn brightly, else He who walks among the golden candlesticks remove our candlestick. Yes, the Church itself needs a season in which to be urged to a deeper devotion and to a holier life, and this too not only for itself, but also for the sake of the world. It needs its missionary spirit to be more deeply stirred and quickened, to be reminded that one of the essential characteristics which it must possess is to be a missionary Church, and that if it fails in this respect it ceases to be a Church; yes, to remember that its only ground of existence, the end for which it was established by the Blessed Saviour and our Lord and God, was that it might go and preach the gospel to, and make disciples of all nations. Deeper internal consecration, and a more intense missionary spirit and zeal are the uses of Lent for the Church, and through it to the world. Only as the Church is true to its character and mission, can the world be evangelized, purified, and brought to the God of heaven and earth, when all the kingdoms of this world shall become the kingdoms of our God and His Christ, and the earth shall be filled with the knowledge of the Lord as the waters cover the sea.

So much then in brief for the use of Lent ; but we see that there may be abuses as well, and the first is the danger arising from the perfunctory use of the season. Indeed we are apt from its annual occurrence to look upon it as a season much as the annual holiday season, when the great exodus abroad takes place, or the annual flight from our larger cities to seaside or mountain resorts, or to quiet secluded country villages. Because of this perfunctory use of the season we yield a very formal conformity to the observances of Lent, and in consequence the services, the modes of discipline are apt to grow isksome. We chafe and fret under them, and instead of deriving good we may derive harm.

Once again, another abuse is that we limit our vision and our purpose. We so often regard the Lenten season as a season absolutely isolated both in time and in its spiritual relations to that portion of our life which precedes or succeeds it. And so from the wildest frivolity or levity we may enter upon the most sober and serious of observances, fasts and discipline, and then when the joyful Easter morn breaks we cast aside all these observances as weeds of which we are only too glad to be rid, and by a renewed or indeed increased wildness of frivolity and levity give no evidence of the deepening of character, the sobering of thought, the elevation of mind, the spiritual communion which we professed to have desired to gain during the holy season.

Ah, friends! It is not the season of Lent which is so much blamed by the world as the inconsistent conduct and character of Christians, who having gone through the austerities and ascetic practices of Lent, come forth no whit better in temper or life. And why? Because of this unwholesome thought of dissociating Lent and its use from the whole of life, from what has gone before, and also from what is to follow. There has been no thickening of spiritual diameter. There has been no gain in holiness. Let it not be so with us. Yes, let me now ask as we stand on the threshold of the last week of Lent—now that we are to enter, as it were, into the dark valley of humiliation, of shame; now as Gethsemane and Calvary and the bitter cross loom in sight— ere this Lent has forever fled let me ask what has been its gain for you? What has this Lent done for you, my brethren? Have you examined your lives more searchingly? have you confessed your sins to God and asked pardon and forgiveness? have you cast out of your hearts old passions and endeavored to cultivate the fruit of the spirit? have you torn from your souls the old hatreds and feuds and angers which have been blackening and blasting them? have you forgiven your enemies? have you striven after holiness? have you been benefited by the services which this holy . season has afforded you? He whom God has placed over you has longed over you and prayed for you that you all might come to know the riches of His love; that you all might come to desire His approval more than aught else; that those of you who have not yet put on Christ may put Him on with sincerity and truth; and that you who have put Him on may be edified and strengthened in your life, adding grace to grace, and virtue to virtue, until we all come in "the unity of the faith, and of the knowledge of the Son of God unto a perfect man unto the measure of the stature of the fulness of Christ."

We have yet one more week of this penitential season, the deepest and most sorrowful and solemn ; let us so use the last remnant of this Lent—the holy week of the Christian year; may it also be of our lives as well!—that we may be ready to enter into the supreme joy of the resurrection morn, and draw near with happy hearts and grateful lives to thank God for His surpassing love; draw near in full assurance of faith, having our hearts sprinkled from an evil conscience, and void of offence towards God and in perfect charity with all men, to the great feast which He will spread before us in the Communion of the Body and Blood of His Son, our Lord and Saviour. Come then with praises and thanksgivings to meet your Risen Lord, who having passed through His shame and humiliation shall then have risen to His glorious triumph and victory over the grave and death—that we too may overcome sin and death, and rise to the new-ness of the risen and glorified life in Him. God grant this blessedness to each of us—and in the end life immortal, and joy in His presence for evermore.